sew z🔘ey

CUT FROM THE SAME CLOTH

written by
Chloe Taylor

illustrated by
Nancy Zhang

Simon Spotlight

New York London Toronto Sydney New Delhi

This book is a work of fiction. Any references to historical events, real people, or real places are used fictitiously. Other names, characters, places, and events are products of the author's imagination, and any resemblance to actual events or places or persons, living or dead, is entirely coincidental.

SIMON SPOTLIGHT
An imprint of Simon & Schuster Children's Publishing Division
1230 Avenue of the Americas, New York, New York 10020
First Simon Spotlight paperback edition March 2016
Copyright © 2016 by Simon & Schuster, Inc.
All rights reserved, including the right of reproduction in whole or in part in any form.
SIMON SPOTLIGHT and colophon are registered trademarks of Simon & Schuster, Inc.
For information about special discounts for bulk purchases, please contact Simon & Schuster Special Sales at 1-866-506-1949 or business@simonandschuster.com.
Text by Caroline Hickey
Designed by Laura Roode
Manufactured in the United States of America 0216 OFF
10 9 8 7 6 5 4 3 2 1
ISBN 978-1-4814-5297-7 (hc)
ISBN 978-1-4814-5295-3 (pbk)
ISBN 978-1-4814-5298-4 (eBook)
Library of Congress Catalog Card Number 2016930257

CHAPTER 1

Secret Socie-TEA!

Hello, readers! I've been doing this blogging thing for a while now, and I've gotten *sew* used to telling you guys everything! But occasionally something happens that's too personal for me to post about. And then I feel funny *not* telling you, because your comments are always helpful and positive and remind me that one of the biggest perks of being a tween fashion designer is having fans who care!

What I'm trying to say is: I got some news that I want to keep a secret for now. It doesn't even have anything to do with fashion—it just relates to me. (That's a "punny" clue, BTW!) However, I'm planning to tell my three very best friends today, and I thought, why not make it an occasion? So we're meeting for tea and scones, and I plan to dress the part, in a full-skirted floral dress with a vintage fedora I got at the thrift store (since I don't have a proper hat for tea)! Wish me luck!☺

Zoey Webber stood outside her favorite café, Tea Time, staring through the glass door. Her older brother, Marcus, had dropped her off, promising to be back in a little more than an hour. She knew she had to go in, but once she did, she'd have to tell her secret, and she didn't know how her friends were going to react. She still didn't even know how *she* felt about the news!

Taking a deep breath, she pulled open the door and strode to the back, where her best friends, Kate

Mackey, Libby Flynn, and Priti Holbrooke, were already seated at a table. Kate was in her customary postsoccer practice warm-ups, Libby looked effortlessly chic in skinny jeans and a ballet-neck top, and Priti—

Zoey stopped in her tracks. "Priti!" she shrieked. "Look at you!"

Priti stood up and did a twirl, giving all of them a chance to take in her purple, gold, and turquoise outfit, and sequined headband. It was very typical of the way Priti *used* to dress, before she'd gone into an all-black clothing phase after her parents' divorce.

"Do you like it?" Priti asked, her cheeks flushed from twirling.

"No, I *love* it," Zoey answered, giving her a hug. For some reason, seeing that her sunny and sparkly friend was back to wearing sunny and sparkly clothes made Zoey feel like all was right in the world again. "Priti, I love you no matter what, but I've missed your rainbow colors."

"Me too," Kate said, "and you guys know I hardly even notice clothes!"

"You *always* look nice, Priti," Libby said diplomatically. "But you look more like you now."

Priti laughed and sat down, pulling out the chair next to her for Zoey. "Thanks, guys," Priti said. "I don't know what happened. I just woke up this morning, and I thought, *Okay, enough with the black clothes already!* So I opened up one of the boxes under my bed with all of my brighter stuff, and it was like seeing old friends. Plus, I've tripled my wardrobe!"

Just then a waiter came by to take their orders. Soon, there were scones and personal teapots for each of the girls.

"To Priti!" Kate said, raising her teacup.

They all clinked cups. Zoey took a sip of her oolong tea. She was spreading clotted cream on a scone when she realized all three of her friends were staring at her.

"What is it? My hat?" she asked, assuming that's what they were looking at.

"It *is* cute," said Libby. "But, um, didn't you have something huge to tell us?"

Zoey blinked. She couldn't believe it. She'd

forgotten the whole reason they'd come for tea because of Priti's bright colors and sequins!

"Oops!" Zoey laughed. "'The power of distraction,' as my dad would say." She paused, and Kate, Priti, and Libby continued to watch her intently. Now that the moment had arrived, Zoey wasn't sure she was ready to share the news.

"Is it about Ezra?" Priti asked breathlessly. The girls knew that Zoey and Libby's friend Ezra had been texting and hanging out. Zoey wasn't sure if she and Ezra were just friends or something more. "Did he *kiss* you?"

Flustered, Zoey stammered, "Um, n-no. Nothing like that. It's not about my love life or lack of one. . . . It's about someone else's."

"Someone else's?" Kate asked. "Whose?"

"My dad's," Zoey said. Her friends' eyes grew large, and Zoey continued, "I finally found out who he's been secretly dating, and not letting me meet, and who wouldn't come to Aunt Lulu's baby shower. And you can't tell *anyone*."

"*And* . . ." Libby prodded her. "You're torturing us!"

Zoey felt her ears get hot. It was still so strange to say it out loud! She leaned in to whisper, "It's Ms. Austen."

The jaws of her friends dropped open. Luckily, none of them had been chewing anything.

"What? You're kidding," Priti said. "Ms. Austen, our *school principal*?"

Zoey nodded.

"Your *dad* is dating our *principal*," repeated Libby. "Wow."

Seeing the shock on her friends' faces was incredibly helpful. Ever since she'd found out, Zoey had been in a state of semi-shock herself. After all, she had a somewhat special friendship with Esther Austen, who'd always been so supportive of Zoey's blog and had made it possible for Zoey and her friend Sean Waschikowski to start the Fashion Fun Club, among other things. Realizing that Ms. Austen had been secretly dating Zoey's father for a while now just made everything feel complicated.

Finally, Kate spoke up. "I guess it makes sense," she said slowly. "I mean, your dad and Ms. Austen probably talked when you had to miss school for fashion-related stuff, and she's so nice. . . ."

Yes, that was how Zoey's dad had explained it. *It just happened,* he'd said.

"And she's got great taste in clothes," Libby added.

"Yes," said Zoey. "And that's *another* weird thing."

Zoey went on to explain that lately, Ms. Austen had been showing up at the house in increasingly casual clothes. Like the past Sunday, when she'd come over early to join the Webbers for their regular Sunday pancake breakfast—the secret ingredients were bacon and blackberries—and had worn work-out clothes with her hair in a messy bun and no makeup on.

"I mean I barely recognized her!" Zoey said.

"That must be so weird," Kate said. "Like when you run into a teacher at the grocery store."

"Hold on! Is our principal going to be your *step-mom*?" Priti asked.

Zoey shrugged. "I don't know, but I think it's getting serious."

"It could be worse," Kate mused. "I mean, at

least you really *like* Ms. Austen. We all do. And you have the fashion stuff in common."

"True," Zoey replied, finishing her scone. "And you know, I *am* glad my dad's happy again. He's been alone for so many years since my mom passed away. But at the same time, I'm kind of annoyed to share him with her and vice versa. I know that sounds selfish."

"It sounds normal," Libby said. "You haven't known for very long, right?"

Zoey shook her head. Her dad and Ms. Austen had told her and Marcus a few months ago, but Zoey didn't want to tell anyone at first.

"It's going to get much easier," Priti said firmly. "And hey, you're kind of lucky. I wish my parents would date people I liked as much as Ms. Austen!"

As always, talking to her friends made Zoey feel better, but she still needed to vent. "Sometimes I just want everything to stay the same, forever!"

Priti patted her arm. "Hey, Zo, change is good. If everything stayed the same, I wouldn't be wearing sequins today!"

When Marcus came to get Zoey, she hugged her friends good-bye. She had to get home to work on a science fair project that was due in a few days.

"Hey, Zo! Did you guys have fun?" Marcus asked.

Zoey smiled. Even though her brother was a few years older, he paid a lot of attention to her and gave her rides. She knew some brothers wouldn't bother to be so nice to a little sister.

"We did," Zoey replied. "And I told them about Dad and Ms. Austen."

"You did?" he asked. "Won't it get around school?"

Zoey shook her head. "No way," she said. "They won't tell anyone. And I needed to be reminded that it's not the worst thing ever."

Marcus laughed. "Of course it isn't, Zoey. It's kind of perfect. And you know, principals are allowed to be happy, too."

"Easy for you to say," Zoey replied. "She's not *your* principal."

"True," Marcus answered. "But she won't be yours for *that* much longer. Anyway, I'm just glad Dad chose someone we get along with."

He was right, of course, but Zoey also thought it was probably normal to struggle with the whole thing. She tried to distract herself by checking her phone for e-mails. She had just opened the mail app when they turned onto their street.

As they pulled into the driveway, Zoey saw a familiar name in her e-mail in-box: Rashida Clarke, from her favorite TV show, *Fashion Showdown*. As she read the message, all her worries faded away:

Dear Zoey:

How are you? It's been too long! I'm writing to tell you that due to a delayed start on our next season of *Fashion Showdown*, we've decided to do a last minute mini-season, just for teens! It'll be called *Fashion Showdown Junior*, and we want you to be a contestant!

It starts ASAP, and the best part is that each episode will take place in a different fashion-forward city around the globe (we start in Paris, then Milan, Tokyo, and Shanghai!), culminating in a runway show in NYC! We'll do all the filming in two trips of about six or seven days each. We hope you'll join us! Have your dad get in touch, and we'll fill him in on all the details.

Fashionably yours,

Rashida Clarke

Zoey dropped her phone into her lap. *Fashion Showdown Junior?* World travel?

"Uh, Zoey?" Marcus asked. "Are you coming inside?"

Zoey looked up and realized they were home and she was sitting in the parked car with her seat belt on. Marcus had already gotten out of the car and was looking at her like she was on another planet. And she was.

"Oh! We're home! Sorry, Marcus," she said. "I have huge news. Where's Dad?"

Zoey and Marcus found their dad in the kitchen . . . with Ms. Austen. Zoey's face briefly fell. She wanted to tell her dad and brother alone and hadn't planned on Ms. Austen being there. It just felt . . . awkward.

Breathing deeply, she said, "Dad, Marcus, Ms. Austen—I have amazing news."

When she told them about the e-mail, Ms. Austen's face lit up immediately.

"Zoey! You're going to be a contestant? I love that show, you know. I've watched it religiously ever since you were a guest judge." Then Ms. Austen came over and hugged her, and Zoey couldn't help feeling warmed by how enthusiastic she was.

Her dad, however, looked a bit shell-shocked. "Missing two weeks of school? Traveling all over the *world*? I can't take that much time off of work. I don't see how this could possibly—"

Ms. Austen put a hand on Mr. Webber's shoulder, cutting him off. "Hang on. We'll figure all that out, I promise. And I'm sure Zoey can do school assignments from the road or catch up when she returns. This is a once-in-a-lifetime opportunity."

Zoey felt immensely grateful to Ms. Austen. Her dad had let her take a few trips to New York with her aunt Lulu, but to get his permission to travel internationally would be nothing short of a miracle.

Her dad took a deep breath. Then he put his arm around Zoey's shoulders. "I'm excited for you, Zoey—I am. I just needed a minute to panic. Let's e-mail Rashida right now and set up a time to talk. And in the meantime, Essie and I are making fajitas, so someone please set the table."

Marcus and Zoey went to get silverware and placemats. As they did, Marcus asked her, "Do you think you'll get to meet a bunch of supermodels on the show? Put in a good word for your big bro?"

Zoey laughed. She was glad he seemed to be recovering after his breakup with Allie Lovallo.

"Will do," she said. "But aren't supermodels sometimes six feet tall? I'll have to stand on a ladder to do fittings! And I don't even know if I can go yet."

But she couldn't help feeling hopeful. Her dad's answer wasn't a firm no, so there was the possibility it could be a real yes. And it was thanks to Ms. Austen.

CHAPTER 2

Vive la France!

You know when you're waiting to hear back about something exciting that *might* happen, but you don't know if it *will* happen, so you're too scared to talk about it or even think about it too much because you don't want to be disappointed? Well, that's me! Believe it or not, I have *another* secret. This one's about a fashion opportunity. This sketch *might* be a clue, and it represents a city I hope to visit some time in the near future . . . but that's all I'm going to say!

In the meantime I *can* tell you about my science fair project, which has been so much fun. I decided to test a theory about whether playing different types of music makes radish plants grow at different rates. I have a control plant that I don't play music for, a country-music plant, a pop-music plant, and a classical-music plant. I've been keeping them in different rooms of the house and then just moving my mp3 player and speaker around the house for thirty-minute "doses" of music for each of them every day for three weeks. The project is due on Tuesday, and believe it or not, there's a clear winner, but I don't want to reveal it yet in case something changes!

On Sunday morning, Zoey lay in her bedroom playing classical music for Plant C when her phone beeped. She reached for it, assuming it was her aunt Lulu checking in to make sure she was still coming over for lunch later to catch up and chat. Instead, she was pleased to find an e-mail from Rashida, in response to the one Zoey and her dad had sent the night before.

Dear Zoey and Mr. Webber,

I'm so thrilled to hear you're interested! And Mr. Webber, don't worry about a thing—I'll call you tomorrow afternoon to go over the details, but our production team is excellent at managing travel, chaperones, sightseeing, and helping with everything from passport issues to packing lists!☺

On another note, we're still casting the show, and we need a few more contestants to get to a total of ten. Do you know of any other clothing designers between the ages of twelve and seventeen? Since our deadline is so tight, we really need to cast the show now. If you know of someone, please send me his or her name!

Rashida

Zoey held the phone tightly, her heart racing. Rashida sounded so confident, like she was sure everything could be worked out. Was it possible that very soon, Zoey might be headed to *Paris*?

Zoey giggled gleefully to herself, unable to control her excitement. The only thing that could make this trip even better would be to have a friend along. She immediately thought of recommending Sean, who led the Fashion Fun Club at school, was the star of home ec, and had saved the day when Zoey needed help finishing her junior bridesmaid's dress for her aunt's wedding. Her friend (and her brother's ex-girlfriend) Allie was also a fashion designer, but she focused on accessories, so Zoey thought she probably wasn't right for the show.

There was no time to waste. Zoey hit reply and began to respond to Rashida's e-mail with Sean's e-mail address and phone number. She decided to wait to tell Sean until she knew Rashida had asked him to be on the show. If Zoey told Sean and Rashida never reached out to offer him a place in the cast, he would be devastated.

Zoey wanted to call Priti, Kate, and Libby right away to tell them about the show, but she wanted to make sure that it was happening. She'd been burned before by things not working out, and if the show got canceled or something, she didn't want certain kids at school to give her a hard time.

But it would take superhuman strength to keep it to herself. Of course, if Rashida got in touch with Sean based on Zoey's recommendation, he would know soon enough, and may be joining her on the show.

She picked up her mp3 player to head down to the dining room to play thirty minutes of pop music for Plant P and to do a little sketching before going to her aunt's house for lunch. After all, she *might* need a few new outfits nice enough to wear in Paris. . . .

Zoey and her aunt Lulu sat across from each other at Lulu's kitchen table, as they had many times before. This time they were having chicken salad sandwiches and couscous, but over the years, they'd spent many happy hours at that table: cutting up magazines, working on mood boards, and discussing ideas for Lulu's interior design business and Zoey's blog. Lulu's kitchen was one of Zoey's favorite places.

Things were different now, of course. Lulu had gotten married, and her husband, John, lived there with her. He was out running errands at the moment, tactfully letting Zoey and Lulu have some girl time. And the biggest change of all, of course, was Lulu's giant pregnant belly.

Lulu rubbed her stomach lightly. "I feel like I'm one hundred years pregnant," she said with a groan. "There's not even room for food anymore!"

Zoey laughed. She had to admit that after not seeing Lulu for a few weeks, she did suddenly look *much* more pregnant. "How long until your due date?" she asked.

"Oh, I've got about seven weeks or so. These things are never exact, I've been told."

Zoey did some mental calculations. *If* she were allowed to go on the two *Fashion Showdown Junior* trips, she'd still be back in time for the birth.

It was Lulu's turn to laugh. "Zoey, I can *see* you counting in your head! Don't worry about it, honey. You can't miss this opportunity for anything."

Zoey had told Lulu—and only Lulu—about the show. She couldn't keep it *completely* to herself. Not surprisingly, Lulu was just as thrilled about it as she was.

"Thanks," Zoey said. "I just hope the producers can talk Dad into letting me go. . . ."

Lulu nodded. "Me too. I think it would be an amazing experience for you. And how lucky that your grandparents made you and Marcus both get passports recently!"

Zoey agreed. Her mother and Aunt Lulu's parents, who lived in Arizona, were planning to take them all to Mexico over the summer and had requested that everyone get passports in advance.

"Let's not talk about the show too much, though," Zoey said. "Because then I'll be disappointed if it doesn't work out. As a matter of fact, I had a real reason for coming over today, and this is it!"

She bent down to pull a neatly wrapped package from her tote bag and passed it across the table to Lulu.

Looking surprised but pleased, Lulu read aloud the tag tied to the package. "'For my favorite new cousin. Love always, Zoey.'"

"Awww, Zoey!" Lulu carefully unwrapped the package to find a beautiful, handmade fabric doll, complete with a dress and bonnet. It had yarn hair, neatly plaited into two braids. "Zoey, I *adore* it!" Lulu exclaimed. She hugged the doll, her eyes filling with tears. A TV commercial had made Lulu cry the last time they were together, and she had explained to Zoey that being pregnant was making her emotional. But Zoey could tell, pregnant or not, her aunt truly loved the gift. "Let's go put it in the nursery right now!" Lulu suggested, wiping her eyes. "C'mon."

Zoey followed her aunt down the hall to the yellow, white, and gray nursery. Lulu placed the doll lovingly on the seat of the glider and then went to the closet.

"I've been organizing!" she told Zoey. "A closet fit for a baby fashionista, don't you think?"

Zoey couldn't believe how tidy everything was. All the outfits she'd made, as well as gifts from the baby shower, were hung on hangers and arranged by size and color. "Wow, Aunt Lulu, you've been busy!"

Lulu smiled and looked around the room. "I know," she said. "Apparently, some moms-to-be go through a nesting phase, when they try to get everything in order. I just don't want to be fussing with laundry when the baby is here."

Zoey smiled too. "That makes sense. And I'm sure he or she will keep you pretty busy for a while!"

"True." Lulu nodded quickly and then looked searchingly at Zoey, as if she were about to ask something important. "I was wondering: Would you like to be sort of a mother's helper for me some days after school or on weekends when your cousin comes, Zoey? It won't be very glamorous—lots of dishes and laundry and holding the baby while I take a shower. But I sure could use your help since John can't take much time off work. Plus, you'd get more quality time with the baby."

Zoey didn't have to think twice. "Of course, Aunt Lulu! I'd love to do that. I can cook a little bit too, if you want. Pancakes and spaghetti, mostly. And grilled cheese."

"That sounds marvelous," Lulu said. "What a lucky baby this will be, to have all of us here to welcome it. Him. Her. It's so hard not knowing!"

Zoey giggled. But inside, she was thinking about how Lulu must have known that Zoey was worried about seeing less of her when the baby arrived. Already, since Lulu had married, things had changed. Uncle John lived there now, and soon, the baby would too. Zoey was sad to say good-bye to some of her traditions, but she was genuinely excited about what was around the corner.

"I'm so excited for you and Uncle John," Zoey said, and meant it.

"Thank you, Zoey," said Lulu. "That means more to me than you know."

--------- CHAPTER 3 ---------

Cute Overload!

Some people might think it's a little strange that I've designed matching outfits for my new cousin and my aunt's dog, but my "canine cousin," Buttons, is like a member of the family! She's my aunt's *other* baby, and therefore, she should have an outfit to match her new human sibling, right? And can't you just imagine some cute pictures of them in their outfits, snuggling together? I've seen so many pictures online of dogs with babies napping on their tummies. It's like the babies think the dog is a huge pillow or something!

I'm also excited to have a tiny person to design things for. Baby clothes are pretty basic to sew, which is nice, and require very little fabric! My aunt told me she could really use some "sleep sacks" for the baby, so I'm going to do some research on baby safety and figure out how to make those. She said they're like little sleeping bags with armholes that zip up and keep the baby warm at night. A lot of parents like to use the sleep sacks instead of blankets, which can get twisted. So that's my next to-do item to help get ready for the baby! Thank goodness I've gotten so speedy at putting in zippers. If any of my readers have other ideas for useful things I could make for the baby, please post in the comments. I'd be *sew* grateful!

By Monday morning, Zoey had bitten off all her nails, waiting for news about *Fashion Showdown Junior*. Her father was scheduled to talk to Rashida later that day, so Zoey was pretty sure she'd know by dinner whether it was a yes or no. Unfortunately, dinnertime felt like weeks away.

She stood at her locker, trying to remember which books she needed to put in her backpack for class, but she was so distracted she could hardly remember her morning schedule. When she felt a hand on her shoulder, she jumped a mile.

"*Sean!*" she yelped. "You scared me to death!"

Sean shrugged impishly and grinned. "It's not my fault you were in outer space. We're at school, you know. Mapleton Prep. Your name is Zoey."

She smiled. "Thanks, Sean."

Then he took a step closer to her, carefully eyeing students as they walked by, as if to gauge whether or not they were listening. "I have to tell you something," he said under his breath.

Zoey's pulse sped up. She had a feeling she knew what he wanted to tell her. "What?"

"*Fashion Showdown Junior,*" he whispered. "They called my parents. Thanks, Zoey—I can't believe you recommended me! That was really nice of you."

"So you're doing it?" Zoey whisper-shrieked.

She looked around also, making sure no one else heard. Their lockers were right off the main hallway at school, and everyone was stopping to get their books and chat with friends.

Sean's face tightened, erasing his usual expression of good humor. "I don't know if I am or not. I'm dying to, but my parents are being weird about it. I didn't even text you about it last night because I'm pretty sure they're going to say no."

"Oh no, Sean, why? Because of all the travel?"

Sean shook his head, his jaw clenched with what looked like anger. "Nah. They don't want me doing a TV show about fashion and sewing. They think everyone will harass me about it."

Zoey was astounded. She'd been in home ec with Sean earlier in the year, and yes, at first some of the other guys had thought it was strange that Sean could sew so well. But once he'd helped them with their projects, and unjammed their machines a few times, they stopped talking about it and left him alone.

"But, Sean, you're the president of the school's Fashion Fun Club. And you helped make the costumes for the musical last year. Everybody knows you sew. . . . I thought all that stuff was kind of over?"

He nodded slightly. "Yeah, well, it is. Pretty much. But I think it's because *Fashion Showdown Junior* is going to be a nationally televised show, and my parents don't want me to be on TV. I don't know. Maybe they think their friends will recognize me on TV and then say things."

Sean's voice was steady, but Zoey knew him well enough to sense how hurt he was. It was one thing to have a parent worried about you traveling the globe and quite another to have both of them worried their friends might disapprove of you doing what you love.

"Maybe my dad can talk to them?" Zoey offered. "Or Ms. Austen? She's really excited about the show."

"Ms. Austen?" Sean asked. "How does *she* know?"

Zoey nearly slapped a hand over her mouth. While she'd told her girlfriends about Ms. Austen and her dad, she still hadn't told Sean, and Zoey intended to keep it that way. "Um, my dad called her about me potentially missing some school days. She was really nice about it."

Sean thought a moment. "Hmm. Well, let me know what your dad decides. If you're officially going, maybe my parents will change their minds."

"I hope so," Zoey said. "And remind them about all the awesome male fashion designers out there! This is an opportunity for you to do something amazing."

Sean sighed, his shoulders drooping slightly. "I know. You're lucky you have such a supportive family, Zoey."

Zoey nodded, realizing she hadn't often stopped to think about that. She just assumed that her dad and Marcus and Aunt Lulu would always back her up because they always had. By now, sewing had become so much a part of her life that she couldn't imagine her family discouraging her from doing it.

"Don't worry," Sean said, eyeing Zoey's crestfallen face. He nudged her playfully with his shoulder, trying to get her to smile. "I haven't given up yet. So you shouldn't either."

Zoey was relieved to see Sean acting like Sean. She nudged him back and grinned. "Good," she said. "Then I won't give up. You, me, and Pair-eeee."

"You mean Paris?"

"In Paris they call it 'Pairrrr-*eee*.' You know, in French?" she joked.

"Well, if by some miracle I do get to go on the show, you can be my translator, 'kay?" Sean smiled.

"*Absolument!*" Zoey agreed, but then saw Sean's confused look and translated for him. "Absolutely!"

Even though she knew her dad wouldn't be talking to Rashida until later in the day, she kept hoping he would call. She knew he was probably just busy at the university, where he was a sports physical therapist, but she couldn't help wonder if his silence meant he had bad news and wanted to deliver it in person.

When she got home from school, she decided to start her homework immediately. Whatever news she got later, she wouldn't be able to focus on her work, so she wanted to finish it early. Marcus went down to the basement to play video games with headphones on so Zoey could study in peace.

When her dad walked in, just after five thirty, the house was so quiet that Zoey nearly jumped out of her skin. She searched her dad's face for clues. But it looked perfectly normal. Not excited or guilty or happy or regretful.

And he was carrying a large pizza box. *Oh well,* she thought. *Even if he says no, at least we get pizza for dinner.*

"How was your day, Zoey?" her dad asked casually, heading into the kitchen as if it were any other day.

Zoey jumped up to follow him. "Dad, do *not* torture me. Tell me what happened on your call! *Please!*" Zoey said "please" so desperately, she even surprised herself.

"How about we eat first," Mr. Webber suggested, going to the sink to wash his hands. "I'm starving."

She couldn't believe how insensitive he was being. "Dad! Seriously?"

Her father smiled but then caught himself. He bit his lip. "Just open the box, Zoey."

Zoey lifted the lid. On top of the pizza, written

out in black olives, were the words "Bon Voyage." Thankfully, Zoey knew that "bon voyage" meant "have a good trip."

"*You mean I can do the show?*" she squealed.

Her father nodded, smiling from ear to ear. "I already signed the contract and e-mailed it." Zoey threw her arms around him, squeezing him tight. "You are the best dad *ever*," she said.

He laughed. "And if I'd said no, would I have been the *worst* dad ever?"

"Well, no," she admitted. "But I would have been soooooo disappointed."

Just then Marcus came upstairs. He stopped and looked at their dad. "She's going?" he guessed. "I could hear that squeal through my noise-canceling headphones!"

Zoey nodded happily. "YES! *And* there's pizza for dinner, so it's great day for all the Webbers!"

Marcus grinned. "How'd Zo talk you into it?" he asked their dad.

Mr. Webber chuckled. "She didn't. When I talked with Rashida today, I grilled her about every possible thing that could happen. But she explained that contestants who don't have an adult family member along with them will always be chaperoned, and that even the sightseeing will be done as a large group. Based on what she told me, Zoey, you might be begging for some privacy by the end of the trip!"

Zoey let out a huge breath. "Privacy, schmivacy," she said. "I'll be sewing all day and then getting judged on TV! I'll be too tired and nervous to care about alone time."

Marcus laughed. "That's probably true." He studied his sister a moment and then said, "I think you're really brave, Zoey, to go on this show. It's going to be hard work, but you can do it."

Zoey was touched. She knew that going on the show was a risk, and that if she did badly, *everyone* at school would probably know about it. Especially kids like Emily Gooding, who seemed intent on proving that Zoey was a no-talent hack. Still, it was nice to know that Marcus believed in her. For the first time, Zoey started to wonder if Sean's parents weren't letting him go because they were afraid he *couldn't* do it. Maybe he needed someone to be in his corner.

"Dad, would you talk to my friend Sean's parents?" she asked quickly. "Rashida asked him to be a contestant too, but his parents are worried about him being on a show about fashion design because he's a boy or something."

Mr. Webber frowned. "Hmm, that's a tough one, Zoey. If they want me to explain why I'm letting you go, I will, but it's not really my place to tell other parents what their kid should or shouldn't be allowed to do."

"But it's so unfair," Zoey pressed. "Lots of guys are fashion designers."

"Honestly, it seems unfair to me too," said Mr. Webber. "Maybe they could call Essie. If they know that the principal is supportive, maybe they'll change their minds. After all, Essie helped me make the final decision today—"

Zoey cut in. "Wait, *Ms. Austen* made the call?"

Mr. Webber nodded cautiously, sensing Zoey's unhappiness. "Well, sort of. I needed another adult's opinion. Someone who wasn't your parent and who could be more objective."

"Why *her*?" Zoey asked. "And not Aunt Lulu?"

Zoey could hear the accusatory tone in her voice, and she didn't like it. She didn't know why she sounded so harsh or felt so annoyed. She knew she should be grateful to Ms. Austen, but she felt like Webber family decisions were none of Ms. Austen's business.

Mr. Webber spoke calmly. "As a matter of fact, I spoke to Lulu today also. But she's rushing to finish several large design jobs before the baby comes . . . and she isn't exactly *objective* when it comes to you, sweetie."

Marcus looked from Zoey to Mr. Webber and then back to Zoey again. "Let's eat," he blurted to break the tension. "This pizza smells too good to sit around getting cold. And this conversation's getting a little too heated, if you know what I mean."

Zoey tried to calm down as they sat down for dinner and Marcus served up the pizza. She took a bite of a slice with the *B* from the word "Bon" and hoped she'd feel better about everything soon. For now, though, her stomach was turning.

CHAPTER 4

Plant Pants!

News flash, Sew Zoey readers: The big fashion secret I couldn't tell you before will be revealed imminently! "Imminently" was a vocab word last week, can you tell? First, I have to tell my best friends in person at school tomorrow.

To tide you over, I *can* tell you about my science fair project results. I have to bring all my radish plants to school today to reveal the winner: It was the classical-music plant, Plant C! To be scientific about it, low-frequency sounds in classical music can activate enzymes and cause plant DNA to replicate, which basically means the sound waves help plants grow. Wish they made me grow too. I wouldn't mind being a few inches taller! But the point is: If you have a garden, try playing a little Vivaldi! I made these plant pants in honor of my experiment and am wearing them today. Aren't they springy?

Zoey maneuvered carefully into school: her four plants packed into the bottom half of a box so they wouldn't tip or spill, and her large poster board and charts tied up together with string and a handle so she could carry them like a briefcase. Marcus had given her a ride to school to make it easier for her to transport her things, but the walk to her locker was precarious.

It was Zoey's first year doing the science fair, and she was excited that her experiment had gone so well. As she made her way to her locker, she was surprised to see kids staring at her and whispering and then turning to chat with one another. Then she heard one person whisper sharply, "Show off." Zoey glanced down at her plants and posters and then at her pants, wondering if people thought her pants were too show-offy. *They're bold, maybe,* she thought, *but no more than usual.*

As she approached her locker, she was surprised to see Kate, Priti, and Libby standing there, looking eerily similar to the kids she'd passed in the hall: standoffish.

"Guys, what's up?" Zoey asked, setting down her things. "Why are you all staring at me like I have five heads?"

"You could have *told* us, Zoey," Priti said accusingly.

"Yeah," Libby added. "I mean, it's a big deal."

Kate didn't say anything, but she wouldn't meet Zoey's eyes and instead stared at the box of plants on the floor.

Zoey was still confused, but she had a feeling her bold pants weren't the problem. "Wait, *what*?"

Just then Sean walked up and said, "Congratulations, Zoey!"

Zoey was still clueless. "I mean, what's the fuss about? It's just a science exper—"

"Um, Zoey," Priti butted in. "What are *you* talking about? We heard you're going to be on *Fashion Showdown Junior*. We're really excited for you, but—"

"But why didn't you tell us?" Kate piped up, her cheeks getting flushed. "We're usually not the *last* to know!"

"Hold on. I haven't told anybody about that. I wanted you to be the f-first to know, I swear," Zoey stuttered. "How *do* you know, anyway?"

Zoey knew there was no way her dad or Marcus or Ms. Austen would have told anyone the news.

"*Sean?*" Zoey turned to him. "Did you . . . ?"

He shook his head. "I only told my parents, I promise. I wouldn't do that."

Priti sighed. "Zoey, seriously? You told Sean and not us that you're going to be on TV and travel all over the *world*? No offense, Sean."

"None taken," he said with a shrug. "But for

the record, I only know about it because Zoey recommended me to be on the show. But my parents probably aren't going to let me, so please don't tell anyone, 'kay?"

Kate reached out and squeezed Sean's arm. "Oh, Sean, I'm sorry! That's awful. And here we are jumping down your throat!"

Zoey was baffled. Who snitched?

"It's all over the news," Priti explained, reading her mind. "I was watching at breakfast, and there was a whole segment about how you're on the spin-off show!"

"And I heard it on the car radio on the way to school," Libby chimed in. "My mom nearly had to pull over, she was so surprised."

"And Priti texted me," Kate said. "Why didn't you tell us yourself? Are you getting too *famous* for us or something?"

Zoey sighed, overwhelmed by how *not* sharing her news had become more of a problem than sharing it. "I'm sorry, guys," she said. "I really am. I've been *dying* to tell all of you, but I wanted to be sure it was actually happening first. My dad just finally agreed *last night* to let me do it! If I'd gotten us excited about it and then not been allowed to go, it would have been too disappointing."

Libby quickly put her arms around Zoey and hugged her. "I knew it had to be something like that," she said. "Sorry if we made it awkward."

"It's okay. I just don't understand how it's all over the news already when I *just* found out I could go!" Zoey knew that being slightly famous meant that sometimes when she was in the public eye there would be backlash from kids at school. But this time it felt like the whole world was talking about her behind her back.

Kate put an arm around her shoulders comfortingly. "C'mon, we've got first period together. I'll walk you there, okay?"

Zoey looked at her gratefully. "Thanks, Kate."

"Keep your head up, Zoey," Sean said. "Remember, everyone is just jealous. Soon, you'll be at *Fashion Showdown Junior*, and none of this will matter."

Fashion Showdown Junior seemed possible, but in that moment, the rest was hard to believe.

It seemed like by second period, every single kid at Mapleton Prep knew Zoey was going to be on *Fashion Showdown Junior* and that she was leaving for Paris in just a few days. Some kids were nice and congratulated her while others just stared. Zoey wished the producers had warned her before the news went public. How much worse would it get when she came back from the trip and the show began airing? And what if she *lost*?

In the middle of her next class, everyone participating in the science fair went to the gym to set up their projects. Zoey was arranging her plants when there was an announcement.

"Zoey Webber," someone said over the loudspeaker, "please come to the principal's office. Zoey Webber, to the principal's office."

All eyes turned to Zoey. She made a mental note to ask Ms. Austen to never, ever call her to the office again.

Then Emily said loudly, "I guess TV stars have more *important* things to do. Explains that sad excuse for a science project."

Feeling fragile, Zoey turned on her heel and was walking away when she heard another voice.

"Emily, we all know *you're* the sad one," Ivy said. "If you had an ounce of Zoey's talent, you'd have better things to do than finding any excuse to pick on her."

Emily was silent and just glared at Ivy, but the rest of the class cheered. The teacher finally noticed the hubbub and told everyone to settle down. Zoey mouthed *Thank you* to Ivy before heading quickly to Ms. Austen's office. Not too long ago, Zoey remembered, Ivy was usually the one doing the teasing, and the idea of her coming to Zoey's defense would have been like something out of the *Twilight Zone*. Luckily, Ivy had changed.

Zoey walked into the main office and was immediately ushered into the principal's office. Ms. Austen looked cool and chic in a melon-colored sheath dress and nude pumps. Zoey was just about to sit down in a chair when she noticed her father was there as well.

"What? Dad!" Zoey exclaimed, startled. "What are you doing here?"

Mr. Webber pressed his lips together, looking grim. "Essie called me and told me the cat was out of the bag with you and the show. She said she'd heard students gossiping about it, and I wanted to make sure you were okay. I also want to yell at those producers for putting you in this position."

Zoey had to admit she was relieved to see her dad. Part of her wanted to run straight into his arms and hide. But she also wondered if people would somehow catch on about her dad and Ms. Austen if they were seen together at school.

"You shouldn't have come here, Dad. I don't want anyone to know you guys are . . . *you know*," Zoey said. "It's bad enough that everyone is talking about me, without them talking about you too!"

Ms. Austen looked slightly embarrassed, but smoothed her dress and said quickly, "Zoey, your dad is here because he's concerned about why the show publicized you being on the show without telling him first. Since you're still a minor, he's worried that it might have been illegal. He wants to call Rashida and thought it might be nice to include you on the call too."

Zoey knew Ms. Austen was trying to say that Mr. Webber was making an attempt to treat Zoey like an adult. But her dad's hard-and-fast rule was that Zoey was allowed to participate in fashion-related events only if she could maintain a normal life at school. Now she wondered if her dad would make her scale back on her fashion design work, since this was definitely not normal. Making her slow down with her fashion work would be worse than anything, even though one day of being the center of attention at middle school was enough to make ordinary life sound pretty great.

"Okay," Zoey said, reeling in her thoughts. "Let's call."

Ms. Austen turned on her speakerphone and called Rashida. Her assistant, Damian, answered.

"Rashida Clarke's office," Damian began, monotone. "Who's calling?"

Ms. Austen motioned to Zoey to speak.

"It's Zoey. Zoey Webber," Zoey said shyly.

"Hi, Zoey!" Damian replied cheerily. "We're getting everything ready for you right now. Visas, hotels, limos—everything. You're going to have the best time, sweetie. But Rashida's in a meeting. Can I help you with something?"

"Thanks, Damian," Zoey replied, feeling slightly guilty. Maybe things were awkward at the moment, she told herself, but it sounded like it would all be worth it.

"Damian, this is Mr. Webber," Zoey's dad spoke up. "Can we speak to Rashida, please? We're having some, uh . . . trouble . . . at Zoey's school because of all the publicity about Zoey being on the show, and frankly, I'm upset that no one ran it by me. At minimum, I would have expected a warning before Zoey's name and picture were released to the public."

Damian murmured an "mmm-hmm." "I understand. I'm afraid the contract *does* state the show has the right to promote itself in any way it deems appropriate, using contestants' names and likenesses, but it sounds like there was a misunderstanding. Let me call Rashida out of her meeting. We don't want you or Zoey, our biggest star, to be unhappy! One moment, please."

Damian put them on hold, and Zoey eyed her

father. She could see the immediate effect the words "biggest star" had on him. It was like all the tension drained from his face and was replaced by beaming pride. It all felt surreal to her.

Ms. Austen noticed also. "Did you know you were the *star* contestant, Zoey?" she asked. "Pretty exciting!"

Suddenly, the stares from Zoey's classmates seemed a lot less important.

Then Rashida's voice came on. "Hello, Mr. Webber?" she said hesitantly. "Damian filled me in. We're so sorry for the miscommunication."

Mr. Webber cleared his throat. "Thanks, Rashida, but my concern is that I had barely told Zoey I'd decided to let her appear on the show," Mr. Webber began, "and she woke up to a different world. She's all over the news. How did it happen so fast?"

Rashida explained that the studio's publicity department had a press release on standby, ready to send out as soon as Zoey's participation in the show was confirmed. When Zoey's dad had e-mailed his official approval, everyone got the green light to promote her on the show. She said that it was a standard form he also signed when Zoey was a judge on *Fashion Showdown*, but that no one realized quite how many news outlets would pick up the story this time around.

"Rashida, this is Essie Austen, Zoey's school principal," Ms. Austen said, introducing herself. "Since it seems this is standard operating practice, can you give us any guidance about how to handle the fallout?"

"Yes, of course. We work with child stars on some other shows, and the truth is, after the first little bit of commotion, things usually settle back down. Her classmates will get used to it."

"That's good to hear," Ms. Austen said, breathing a sigh of relief.

Rashida went on. "I'm sorry if this caught you all a bit off guard. In the future I'll be happy to keep you more in the loop when we have something coming out, so you can prepare for it. How's that?"

"That would be great," Mr. Webber said. "I want Zoey to be able to take advantage of opportunities like this, but not at the expense of her education and, well, her seminormal childhood."

"Of course," Rashida agreed quickly. "But I think I should tell you that you have a *very* talented daughter. We think this is just the beginning for her. You might want to look at this as practice for things to come."

Zoey felt her heart skip a beat. She still sometimes felt like she'd just had a lot of good luck so far, and that any time now, her luck would dry up and she'd just be a regular kid who sewed as a hobby. But Rashida didn't think so—Rashida, who produced the most successful fashion reality show on TV.

After they'd said their good-byes and hung up, Mr. Webber grabbed a tissue from Ms. Austen's desk and patted his forehead, as if he'd been sweating.

"Are you . . . okay?" Zoey asked.

Mr. Webber nodded. "I just want to protect you, honey. I know this is just the *beginning* of you growing up, but I thought I had a few more years of you being my little girl before I had to send you out into the world."

Zoey grinned. "You do, Dad! I'm still in middle school. And even though I'm excited for this big trip, I'm also worried I might get a little homesick, being so far away."

Mr. Webber winked at her. "I won't let my girl be homesick. You'll get so many e-mails, texts, and video chats from me, you'll be begging me to leave you alone!"

"I hope so," Zoey said, and meant it.

CHAPTER 5

Totally Toga!

And now for the spilling of the beans! *Finally*, I can tell you all that I'm going to be a contestant on a special mini-season of my favorite show, *Fashion Showdown*! But I have a feeling you already knew that since it's literally been all over the news. We start filming *Fashion*

Showdown Junior this coming weekend in Paris, and then we head to Milan *(that's in Italy, cough, cough)*. Then we fly home so we don't fail out of school, and two weeks later we head to Tokyo and Shanghai. But in each place, one contestant will be eliminated and will be out for the rest of the show. Then after four challenges in four cities, the six remaining finalists will get to compete in a real runway show in NYC!

I haven't had much time to plan for this whirlwind world tour, but I have been thinking about the cities we'll be visiting. I don't know anything about modern Italian fashion, but I know that ancient Romans wore togas, which basically looked like white bedsheets beautifully draped around them. I'd like to make a toga in really bright colors, like magenta and purple, for a change, and add metallic accents with gold or silver thread, or beading. Metallics work with just about everything! (Right, P?)

I've also been thinking about how I'll perform under pressure. Not to toot my own horn or anything, but I'm kind of used to sewing complicated projects in zero time, like when I made my aunt's wedding dress. But, come to think of it, that didn't turn out as *perfectly* as

I'd hoped (a seam ripped during the reception), and I was really stressed out the whole time.

I think I'm more nervous about all the long flights than anything: It's my first time going abroad! Any travel tips?

As she entered school on Wednesday, Zoey was relieved to see that most kids seemed less interested in her than they'd been the day before. There were still some hushed whispers and pointed looks, but people appeared to have moved on to talking about other things, like tests and basketball games. Zoey strolled to her locker without feeling like she had to hurry past everyone to avoid the gossip. Her phone buzzed as she was getting her books, and she pulled it out of her pocket.

It was a text message from her friend Ezra.

Congratulations on Fashion Showdown Junior! I guess I have to keep up with you by reading your blog now, eh, big TV star?

Zoey cringed. She'd love to go one day without annoying someone for not sharing her news. She had just posted the news to her blog right before she left for school, so she guessed Ezra must read it pretty frequently to have seen it. She was flattered he read her blog, but she felt guilty she'd forgotten to tell him yesterday when the news had broken. Since Ezra was at a different school, they didn't see each other every day, but still, she hadn't even thought of texting him!

So sorry! she wrote back. **It all happened so fast. I leave this Saturday. Can you believe it?**

Immediately, a text bubble appeared, showing that he was replying.

Can we hang out before you go? Ice cream after school tomorrow?

She wrote back, **Sure! Meet you there.**

The bell rang, and Zoey tucked her phone into her backpack. With a smile on her face, she floated to class. She had an ice-cream date with Ezra, and her first trip to Europe was in just a few days. It was turning out to be a *very* good week.

In English class, Zoey often chatted with her friend Gabe Monaco, who was a novice photographer. He was supernice, and very talented, and always asked

Zoey what she was working on. So she wasn't surprised to see him perched on her desk when she walked into class, apparently waiting for her.

"Hi, Gabe!" she said. "What's up?"

His eyebrows shot up. "With me? Nothing! But something's always up with *you*, Zoey Webber. I didn't get a chance to tell you yesterday since you weren't in class: Congrats!"

Zoey felt her cheeks turn pink, and she quickly bit her lip to keep herself from breaking into a huge, beaming smile. She and Gabe had been friends for a long time, and a few months ago she'd started to think of him as a bit more than a friend, especially after he'd helped out at her Aunt Lulu's wedding at the last minute and was the wedding photographer for the day. But a French student, Josie, who'd recently flown back home to France after months of living with her American relatives, was his girlfriend at the time. *I like Ezra now,* she reminded herself, and even though she wasn't really clear on where they stood, there was no reason to act all weird around Gabe. But she still felt weird.

"So, Zoey," Gabe began, and then chuckled at

his pun. "Well, I was wondering if you'd let me do a photo essay about your experience on the show."

Puzzled, Zoey asked, "Hmm . . . what do you mean exactly?"

Gabe leaned forward excitedly, eager to explain. "Well, most middle schoolers don't star on a reality TV show. It's a huge deal. And I thought I could get some photos of you—packing, at the airport, or whatever—to document the experience. You know, for the school newspaper."

"Um, I don't know," Zoey said cautiously. Just the idea of Gabe putting photos of her, possibly looking scared and nervous, into the school newspaper made her wary. "What if . . . I mean, what if kids just think I'm full of myself for getting my picture taken or something?"

Gabe shook his head. "No, I'll be really careful, Zoey. I won't print any pictures that would make you uncomfortable or make it look like you're, you know, stuck-up or anything. Because you're *not*," he added emphatically.

Zoey hesitated for another second. But then,

remembering how much she trusted Gabe, and how he really came through for her aunt on her wedding day, Zoey agreed, with one condition.

"Okay," she said. "We've got a deal! As long as you give me a few copies for my dad. He'd love that."

Gabe grinned widely. "Of course! I can even make an album. So, I can come by your house and get some shots of you packing whenever you're ready."

Zoey felt her heart sink suddenly, realizing there might be *another* person hanging around Zoey's house that she'd forgotten about: Ms. Austen. And she did *not* want Gabe to see the principal at the Webber house and guess what was going on! She made a mental note to tell her dad when Gabe was coming by to make sure that Ms. Austen wouldn't be there.

"Right, my house," she replied at last. "Sounds good."

The bell rang, and Zoey plopped down in her seat. She wanted to put her head in her hands and groan. Things had never been more complicated!

Zoey dressed with care for school on Thursday, knowing she'd be heading straight to the ice-cream parlor afterward to meet Ezra. She wore a great wrap skirt she'd made from an anchor-print fabric, with a tucked-in striped tee. Then she added super-pointy flats with cat faces on them. At school, she had Priti do her hair in a fishtail side braid. When she finally pushed through the door of the ice-cream parlor and saw Ezra there, sitting at a table for two in the corner, she realized just how nervous she was. She didn't know what to expect or what she wanted to happen.

Zoey went over to him and was surprised when he stood up and gave her hug. To her, it felt like he held on for a few seconds too long, but then decided she was probably just feeling awkward about their quasi-date, and sat down.

It was then that she noticed he'd already gotten them each a hot-fudge sundae, complete with nuts and a cherry.

"Um, is this for me?" she asked.

He looked pleased, joining her at the table. "Yeah, remember? At Libby's Bat Mitzvah, they had that sundae bar, and you thought it was so neat. I got you the biggest one on the menu."

Zoey nodded. She did remember—she *had* thought it was neat, but she had really wanted a cone and, well, to pick out her own flavors. She realized Ezra was trying to be nice, so she smiled enthusiastically, picking up her spoon.

"Thanks, Ezra!" she said. "That was really thoughtful of you."

"I'm just glad you didn't get here late, or it would have been ice-cream soup," Ezra joked. "I should have thought ahead."

Or let me order for myself, Zoey thought. But they both started eating, and Ezra asked her questions about the show. Zoey tried to answer them as best she could, but there were still a lot of things she didn't know, like how exactly they were going to have the episodes ready to air so fast, in a little over a week.

"I can't wait to watch you on TV," he said. "And tell people I know you!"

Zoey grimaced. "You may not want to," she said. "Depending on how I do. There are going to be lots of designers there and—" Zoey stopped midsentence, picturing herself totally freezing up on TV, unable to come up with any ideas while the other designers around her churned out one fantastic outfit after another.

Ezra must have noticed the look on her face because he reached over and touched her arm. "Zoey, what is it?"

"Um, I just hadn't really thought about the competition." She tried to laugh it off and shrugged. "I've been so caught up in getting my dad's permission to go at all!"

Ezra cleared his throat and wiped his hands off with his napkin. He'd finished his sundae already while Zoey was still digging away at hers. "I, uh, got you something," he said. "You know, for good luck."

And from behind his back he produced a tiny wrapped package.

Zoey was a bit taken aback. "A present?"

Ezra nodded. "Don't worry. It's really small, something to take with you for good luck."

Ezra really was thoughtful. Zoey felt guilty that she hadn't even remembered to tell him about her big trip, and he'd still gone out and gotten her a gift!

Cautiously, she ripped open the paper and lifted the lid off the box.

Inside was a tiny enamel airplane, about the size of a paper clip.

"Aw, thanks, Ezra," she said, but she didn't quite understand what it was.

Ezra could tell she was confused and hurried to explain. "It's a good-luck charm for your bracelet," he said. "And I picked an airplane because you're 'going places'!"

Zoey's face broke into a smile, and she held the airplane up, examining it. Now, she could see the link attached that made it a charm.

"Thank you, Ezra," she said sincerely. "This is *exactly* what I needed."

On Friday afternoon, Zoey invited Kate, Libby, and Priti over to help her pack for Paris and Milan. She'd be gone for about a week, so she needed a decent amount of clothes, but contestants were limited to one carry-on and one piece of checked luggage only.

That meant she had to be very selective about what she brought.

The girls were all in Zoey's room, sharing a plate of pretzels and hummus and voting on items as Zoey pulled them out of her closet. Her dad's largest suitcase was open in one corner of the room, already half full.

"This?" asked Zoey, holding up a flowy peasant dress, which had been her mother's. It was one of her favorites.

"Yes," Priti said immediately. "You can wear it with boots or flats. Perfect for Italy!"

Zoey folded it carefully and placed it into the suitcase. Next, she picked up a dark-gray pleated skirt.

Kate frowned, scooping up some hummus with a pretzel. "Do you really need a bunch of fancy stuff? I mean, won't you mostly be in the workroom sewing? I'd just bring jeans and some T-shirts."

Libby laughed loudly. "I know that's what *you'd* wear, Kate, and be gorgeous in it. But Zoey's going to be on TV! And when has she ever just worn jeans and a T-shirt?"

Kate flashed a smile. "Almost never, I guess."

"You're going to need more tops," said Libby. "Bring that cute black wrap sweater you have, with the ruffle in the front."

"No way," said Priti. "You need colors so you'll stand out from the other contestants! Bring your purple top, and that blue one, and your red-pink-and-yellow dress that I love."

Kate shook her head. "I just think she won't need *quite* so many things for one week."

Priti nodded reluctantly. "Hmmm . . . Kate does have a point. And if you want to buy fabulous clothes in Europe, you'll need to leave some room in your luggage to bring things home."

Zoey's head was beginning to spin. She looked over at her suitcase, which had seemed so big when she'd gotten it down from the attic, but it was filling up fast. "You know, maybe I'll just bring a few of my favorite things and a few neutrals to mix and match with them."

Zoey carefully folded up some leggings, tunics, and skirts that were all neutral, left in her favorite bright pieces, and took out the clothes that were less practical for marathon sewing sessions.

"Hey, what's that?" Libby asked, pointing to the bracelet on Zoey's wrist. "Is that plane charm new?"

Zoey felt both a little embarrassed and a little excited to explain where she'd gotten it. "Yeah, it's uh, a good-luck charm. From Ezra."

All the girls gasped in unison, and it was so funny, Zoey burst into giggles. "You should see your faces!" she exclaimed. "It's an enamel airplane, not an engagement ring."

Priti began waving her hands around excitedly. "I know, but *still*. He must really like you."

Libby agreed. "That was *very* sweet of him."

Zoey nodded. She agreed; it was sweet. "It's just . . ." Zoey couldn't quite find the words to express how she felt about the gift. And the ice-cream date. She'd been thinking about it ever since, and something just didn't feel right.

She looked at Kate, sensing that Kate might understand.

"You don't really know how you feel about him," Kate guessed. "And he seems to like you a whole lot, and that makes you *really* unsure, because you like him too, but maybe just as a friend, and the gift and attention make you uncomfortable."

It was Zoey's turn to gasp. "How did you know? That's it *exactly*."

Kate smiled ruefully. "Because that's how it was with Tyler. He was such a cool person, and I had so much fun talking with him. But he seemed to like me so much, you know, *that* way, and it just made me want to be friends only or stop hanging out. It sounds weird, but it's true."

"It does sound weird," Priti agreed. "Ezra and Tyler are both really cute, nice guys. Why wouldn't you like them back?"

Zoey shrugged. "It's not that I don't like him," she explained. "It's just that it's a little too intense or something. I mean, he ordered ice cream for me yesterday, even though he didn't know what I wanted, and he got me this gift, and I think he reads my blog *every* day!"

It was Libby's turn to shake her head. "I agree with Priti. It sounds pretty fun to me, except maybe the part about him ordering for you. But if you're not into him, maybe you should just be friends."

Zoey chewed her lower lip. "I think I need to put this decision on hold." There was too much going on. When she returned from the trip, she'd make plans with Ezra and see how she felt. For now, though, Gabe was coming over soon to take photos while she finished packing.

"Zoey!" Mr. Webber called up from downstairs. "I'm going to order Chinese food for dinner. Would your friends like to join us?"

Zoey waited for everyone to respond.

"Um, *obviously*," said Priti. "We still have so much to do! And no one has mentioned my new sparkly tee yet. My mom gave me her credit card the other day to buy some new things because she's so happy I'm out of my 'dark phase,' as she called it."

"I love it! Can I bring it on my trip?" Zoey joked.

Priti nodded solemnly. "Yes, you can. If you promise to mention me on TV and say that I'm the best, most *wonderful* friend in the universe."

Zoey and the other girls laughed. "Seems fair!"

----------- CHAPTER 6 -----------

Totally Travel-rific!

This is the outfit I've put together for my long flight to France. I made the pants with elastic in the waists and cuffs, so they're comfy enough to sleep in. And the fabric is a blend that hardly ever wrinkles! My shrug will keep me warm, but it isn't too warm, and my shirt says that I'm a star. (That was my dad's idea. I actually feel kind of silly about it, but he insisted.)

I'm *so* ready for this trip to begin. I can't wait to get stamps on my passport! We fly overnight to Paris, stay a few days, and then take a quick flight to Milan. I'm bringing my sketchbook on the plane, to start brainstorming ideas for things I can make during the challenges. Maybe none of them will work out with the materials or challenges they give us, but at least it'll keep me busy and give me *something* to start with. I went to sleepaway camp last summer, so I've been away from home before, but I've never been to a foreign country! I'm trying to be brave, but I really have no idea what to expect.

My friends all ended up staying late last night before wishing me farewell, including my pal G. He's a talented photographer and is doing a photo essay about my *Fashion Showdown Junior* experience, so he documented the packing madness. I leave tonight, and since it's an overnight trip, my dad is insisting I take a quick power nap now. So see you next time . . . in Paris!

Zoey woke to someone shaking her shoulder. She'd been so deeply asleep, she had a hard time getting her eyes to focus on the face. It was her dad.

"Zoey," he said. "*Chérie,* time to get up. We have to leave for the airport."

"The airport?" Zoey repeated. Her brain was foggy and her limbs felt heavy, as if she were glued to the bed. "Why?"

Her father laughed. "Zoey, this is it! Paris! Fashion! Showdown!"

Zoey shook her head to clear the cobwebs and then felt a sudden sense of panic.

"I'm not ready!" she said.

"Yes, you are, honey," he said firmly. "Just freshen up and come downstairs so Marcus can say good-bye before he leaves for his SAT prep class."

Zoey splashed some water on her face and then checked her travel outfit in the mirror quickly. "I'll be in *France* tomorrow," she said to herself, shaking her head in disbelief.

At the front door, Marcus hugged her, pulled back, and held on to her shoulders for a moment. Looking her right in the eye, he said, "Now listen, Zoey—remember, this is a competition. Don't get distracted by the TV cameras or the other contestants or the pressure. Just focus on your work and make your best outfits ever. I'll be proud of you no matter what, but I also know you can win!"

Zoey knew that on every season of *Fashion Showdown*, one or two contestants got overwhelmed by the time limits or the competition, and simply froze. She didn't want that to happen to her.

"I'll do my absolute best," she promised Marcus. "And I'll be proud of you no matter how you do on the SATs. But I also know you'll do great!"

He nodded and walked out the door. As he was getting into his car, he waved good-bye, and Zoey felt a pang in her heart. Even though it was a short trip, she'd miss her big brother. Zoey, Marcus, and their dad were such a small family that when one of them was gone, everything felt off. She knew they would miss her, too. She was glad she'd told Gabe not to come and shoot today. She was way too emotional!

"I'm ready," she told her father.

Her dad loaded her luggage into the car, and Zoey climbed into the front seat.

"Dad," she said tentatively as they got onto the freeway. "I think I just realized that *tomorrow I'm going to be on a reality TV show.*"

Her father laughed. "You sure are!" He hummed and tapped his fingers on the steering wheel, as if everything were perfectly ordinary.

"It was so much easier when I was a judge on the show. What will everyone think if I don't do well in the competition?" The butterflies in Zoey's stomach had begun flapping with surprising force.

"Take a deep breath," said her dad. "Remember, we all love you no matter what."

Zoey believed him, but she wondered if kids at school would give her endless grief if she didn't do well. Kids like Emily. She had to smile, though, when she thought about Ivy and how Ivy had defended her, but she began to worry about something else.

"Dad, what if the other contestants on the show don't like me?"

Her father exhaled deeply. "Well, if I've learned anything over the years it's that you can't control what people think of you, so you might as well just be yourself and enjoy the experience, okay?"

Zoey nodded. "Okay, I know you're right, Dad. I just think it would be easier if I had a friend along. You know, since I'll be so far away."

Her father gave her a funny smile and steered the car toward the exit for the airport.

At the airport, Zoey's dad helped her check-in at the ticket counter but couldn't go through security with her. The show had arranged for Rashida and the adult chaperones to meet the contestants and make sure they were well taken care of on the flight.

"Do you see anyone?" Zoey asked anxiously as they approached the security line.

"Rashida said she'd be here early," her father muttered, scanning the crowd.

Then, out of nowhere, a familiar person in a checkered shirt came running toward Zoey. It was her friend Sean, and he was holding a carry-on bag. His smile was a mile wide.

"Sean?" Zoey squealed. "Wait, really? *How?*"

She threw her arms around his neck and hugged him. She was thrilled Sean's parents had agreed to let him be on the show, but she was also relieved that Mapleton Prep would be represented by *two* contestants. It wouldn't feel so much like all eyes were on her.

Zoey turned to her dad. "Did you know?"

He nodded. "It's a recent development, but we thought it would be fun to surprise you."

Sean's eyes glowed, and he looked happier than Zoey had ever seen him. "Can you believe it? Ms. Austen called my parents and said I was doing really well in French class and thought the trip would be great for my language skills," he whispered as his mom and dad came up behind him. "And she reminded them it was a fully paid, around-the-world trip and that fashion design is a huge business and could turn into a career."

"You're kidding," Zoey whispered back.

Sean shook his head.

Zoey was amazed. Somehow, Ms. Austen had found the exact right thing to say to the Waschikowskis. Zoey felt she owed Ms. Austen a huge thank-you and decided to bring her back an especially nice souvenir.

Mr. Webber talked to Sean's parents for a few

minutes before Rashida found them and said it was time to take Sean and Zoey through security.

Zoey could tell her father wasn't quite ready to let go of her yet because he didn't answer Rashida. He just stood there blinking at her.

Rashida must have understood because she said, "Mr. Webber, Mr. and Mrs. Waschikowski, I'll guard Zoey and Sean with my life, and so will the other chaperones. They've already headed in with the other contestants, though, so we have to go. Grab your passports and boarding passes, kids, and we'll get in line."

Zoey gave her dad one last, long hug and then followed Sean and Rashida into the security line.

"I love you!" she yelled to her father, who was standing there, watching her go.

"I love you, Zo!" he called back.

Sean squeezed her arm, and Zoey nearly started crying. She was so happy to have her friend with her.

——— CHAPTER 7 ———

All-Night Flight . . .

Wow! I can hardly believe I survived the flight! It was about seven and a half hours, and I slept for some of it, but mostly I sketched and talked to S. Wait—you guys don't even know my friend S is on the show! Ha! It was a surprise to me too, and it's such a huge relief to have a pal in my corner. Friendship and fashion definitely go together.

Our group arrived in Paris early this morning (in Parisian time, the middle of the night back in the States!), and we were taken to our hotel to drop off luggage, change clothes, and have a bit of downtime. I have my own bedroom in a suite with other contestants, and it's really nice, but it sounds like we'll be in the workroom most of the time. The first challenge starts soon, and we'll be sewing all day!

I sketched this outfit on the plane when I couldn't sleep, and then I saw a few French women on the way to the hotel wearing midi skirts like the one in my sketch. Seems like a good sign, right? Time to go, so wish me luck, or *"bon chance"* as they say here!

After a quick outfit change, Zoey went down to the lobby to meet Sean. Several other contestants were also there, waiting and chatting with one another. One, a petite girl with a messy brown bun and a pair of authentic-looking cowboy boots, introduced herself as Leanne. Another girl, who looked like she might be around Marcus's age, had dyed hair the color of red Kool-Aid and was named Cat.

"So, is this your first time in Paris?" Cat asked Zoey and Sean.

Zoey nodded. "It's my first time anywhere!" Zoey told her. "I can't wait to see the Eiffel Tower and the Jardin de Tuileries."

"The whole city's amazing," Cat said. "I came on a student exchange last summer."

"Milan is great too, though," Leanne said. "My dad's Italian, and he took me a few years ago."

When neither Sean nor Zoey replied, Leanne looked them both over carefully. "How young are you guys?" she asked.

"We're both in middle school," Sean answered with just the right amount of confidence.

Zoey was relieved he'd answered. She knew she would have stuttered and sounded embarrassed in front of these two older girls who seemed so worldly.

"Wow," said Cat. "You must be pretty good, then." She winked and motioned to the door, where a large bus had pulled up with a *Fashion Showdown Junior* sign in its window. One of Rashida's assistants began corralling them onto the bus, and minutes later they were riding through the streets of Paris.

Zoey wished the ride would go on forever. She loved the narrow streets, sidewalk cafés, and amazing window displays. It was still early morning, but people were out and about, heading to work, meeting for breakfast, stopping for croissants at *boulangeries*. She couldn't wait to get out and explore.

Too soon, they crossed a bridge onto an island and the bus stopped.

"This is Île de la Cité, which means City Island," Cat explained, turning to point at a huge cathedral. "And that is the Notre-Dame, one of the most famous cathedrals in the world."

Zoey was awestruck by the enormous gothic structure, full of stained-glass windows, gargoyles, and arched supports that Cat said were called "flying buttresses." Zoey couldn't quite stifle a laugh at the phrase.

"Funny, right?" admitted Cat. "But that's what my architecture teacher said they're called."

Soon, they were walking into a large stone

building across from the Notre-Dame that looked several hundred years old. Zoey looked for Sean and noticed him chatting up ahead with a boy named Todd, who looked to be about fourteen or fifteen years old. There were so many new faces, and Zoey was getting really curious about their sewing and designing skills.

The contestants were led up an old staircase to a bright workroom with big windows facing the Notre-Dame. The room had ample workstations for each contestant, with shiny sewing machines and stacks of sketchpads and pencils. On one wall there were several shelves holding things like scissors, trim, and notions. On another were shoes, jewelry, hats, and other accessories. It was a sewing dreamland.

Rashida stepped to the front of the room. "Welcome to *Fashion Showdown Junior*! I know you must be jetlagged, but hang in there because in just a moment, we're going to begin filming our first challenge. I know it's fast, but we want to hit the ground running. Does anyone have questions?"

Everyone was quiet, and Zoey wondered if they

were as excited and nervous—and tired—as she was. She settled herself at the nearest workstation and tried to force her brain to wake up.

Rashida went over some rules about how everything would work and what to do if there was a problem. As she talked, the camera crew streamed into the room, adjusting the lights, setting up the boom, and wheeling in several large cameras. Meanwhile, a makeup artist quickly freshened up the older girls' makeup; applied natural-looking lip gloss, blush, and powder to the younger girls' faces; and insisted on powdering the boys' faces too, so they wouldn't look shiny on camera.

When it was Zoey's turn, she asked the makeup artist if she could use her own lucky lip gloss. It was a gift from Daphne Shaw, her fashion fairy godmother, when Zoey was a judge on the original *Fashion Showdown*, and she had made sure to bring it to Paris. The makeup artist agreed, dabbed some on Zoey's lips, and headed to the next contestant.

That was when Rashida pulled Zoey aside. "Zoey, everyone you worked with on *Fashion Showdown* wants you to know how happy we are that you're here, and they wish you luck. Myself included," she said. "They all want to come say hi, but we have to treat you like the other contestants to make sure things are fair, especially with the judges. Okay?"

Zoey nodded. "I get it," she said.

Rashida whispered "good luck" and ducked out of the way as the countdown to filming began.

Someone yelled, "Action!" Then the host of the show, Oscar Bradesco, appeared. He quickly explained how the mini-season would work and then gave the orders for their first challenge. Zoey made notes on her sketchpad, so she wouldn't forget anything.

All ten contestants would be given the same two fabrics to use: one bold print and one plain. The challenge was for each of them to make an outfit with these fabrics that showed their skills, creativity, and personal style. They had eight hours to work today, and a few more the next day, followed by a runway judging in the afternoon. Real models were going to wear the outfits on a real runway!

Sean, who sat one table away from Zoey,

muttered, "Wow, they weren't kidding about this being a 'fast production,' huh?"

Zoey nodded but didn't speak. Her mind was already whirling with possibilities as she received her allotment of the two kinds of fabric. One was a geometric print, and the other was an iridescent solid that tied into the printed fabric. Such a striking print, however, almost guaranteed that most of the outfits would look similar.

Zoey began sketching, focusing mostly on pieces she knew she could sew well, and quickly, and that felt like her style.

About an hour later she began to cut her fabric to fit her model's measurements. As she worked, she couldn't help overhearing Oscar checking in with Sean, whom Zoey had noticed had zoomed ahead and was already sewing a dress. She felt bad for even thinking it, but she thought it looked kind of boring, especially for someone with Sean's quirky fashion sense.

Oscar and Sean had a quiet conversation, with a camera right in Sean's face. Zoey could see his cheeks were slightly red.

"You don't *have* to do a dress, you know," Oscar was explaining to Sean. "Any type of outfit show-casing your style is allowed."

Sean looked frustrated but kept his cool. When Oscar and the camera had moved away to a girl named Ellen, who had a cute, blond pixie haircut, Zoey scurried over to him. "Sean, what's wrong?"

He shook his head. "It's just . . . I haven't designed much stuff by myself, Zo. I can sew really well and make costumes and follow a pattern. But I don't really have big ideas for my own designs. So I just cut out a dress. And I don't even like dresses!"

"Then try and do something else!" Zoey suggested. "There's time. Not a lot, but there's time."

"But I've already cut the fabric, and we don't get more," Sean explained. He was whispering so softly, she could barely hear him. "And all these cameras are making me nervous."

"It gets easier. Soon, you'll forget the cameras are there," Zoey said. She hated to see Sean so stressed. Not when she knew how badly he wanted to be there! And someone would get voted off tomorrow. She couldn't let it be Sean. "If you really want to start over, maybe you could cut the fabric into strips and then layer them on muslin to make anything you want," she suggested.

Sean's spirits seemed to lift. "Great idea! Thanks, Zoey."

Zoey returned to her station and got to work on her own project. The clock seemed to move relentlessly, with another hour gone every time she picked up her head. She couldn't decide if she wanted more time or less, so she could go to sleep sooner. Plus, for some reason, their workroom was freezing, so Zoey was both tired and cold. Sean noticed her chattering teeth and offered her his cashmere sweater-vest, which she layered over her outfit. It looked a little odd, but she was grateful.

Finally, it was time to stop for lunch and a break. Since the contestants were considered child actors, they were only allowed to work a certain number of hours at a time before scheduled downtime.

Zoey wolfed down lunch—cheese on a baguette, and a yummy, fizzy orange drink called Orangina—so she could take a quick nap. But when Sean asked her for advice on how to fix part of an armhole, she helped him instead and didn't get a chance to nap.

Soon, the end of their workday approached. Zoey had made a swingy tank top and a pair of high-waisted shorts. She was happy with the overall look, but it still needed excellent finishing work to look good on the runway.

When the bell rang signaling the end of the challenge, Zoey felt ready to collapse. She'd barely slept on the plane, even though Rashida had told them to sleep since they'd be starting filming soon after landing in Paris. It had been just too exciting.

Zoey overheard some of the other contestants making plans to meet in the common room when they got back to the hotel, to hang out and order food.

"Are you going to go?" Sean asked Zoey.

Zoey shook her head. All she wanted to do was e-mail her dad and Marcus and give them a quick update, take a hot shower, and go to bed. "I'm so tired, and I still have so much to do tomorrow!"

"Me too," said Sean. "But I feel much better about my outfit for the challenge. Thanks for saving me, Zoey! You're a true friend."

Zoey, who was still wearing his sweater-vest, said, "Believe me, Sean, I need you just as much as you need me!"

Zoey woke up the next morning feeling almost normal. She'd slept almost eleven hours! She quickly answered a few e-mails from her family, Kate, Libby, and Priti, and she was happy to see that her aunt Lulu had sent her a good-luck e-card.

Today was her first judging! It was a big day, and she wanted to dress right. Remembering how cold it had been while they were working yesterday, Zoey opened her suitcase, hoping she'd packed a thick, wooly sweater instead of one light shrug. Unfortunately, she hadn't planned on an arctic freeze in the workroom.

Oh well, she thought. *I guess I'll just have to put* everything *on!*

And with that, she began layering on clothes, reasoning it would be easy to remove a layer later if she was too warm. She wore a pair of black leggings; a pleated skirt; a long-sleeve shirt with a tank over it, worn like a vest; and then on top—a knit cowl she'd made when she'd taught herself to knit a few months before. It wasn't the most chic outfit ever, but she'd be warmer than yesterday, and be able to focus on her work instead of on shivering.

She took extra time brushing her hair, and put on earrings. Then, with a last look in the mirror, she crossed her fingers and wished herself luck.

Back in the studio the contestants would have an hour to work and then an hour to meet with their models for a fitting, and then some time to make alterations while the models got their hair and makeup done. With the judging just a few hours away, Zoey got to work, trying to make sure the waist of the shorts was lying flat and not puckered, and the swingy top had the right movement to it.

"Zoey—help!" Sean called.

Zoey, who was right in the middle of fixing a seam, felt a momentary fit of frustration. Being interrupted at this stage could have really messed things up. But she stopped her machine and then stepped over to his station. "What's up?"

"I still can't get this armhole to work," he said.

Zoey looked at the garment, which was a sporty one-shouldered top, and realized the fabric had been cut a bit too short on one side. "You'll have to just tighten up the whole armhole and hope the model has a small arm," she said.

Zoey got back to work and was amazed when only a few minutes later, the models came in. There was still so much to do!

Zoey's model was from Martinique and about fifteen years old. Her name was Anne-Thérèse, and she had dark brown hair, honey-colored skin, freckles, and a bright smile.

"You have made a lovely outfit," Anne-Thérèse said in perfect English. "I would wear this anywhere!"

"*Merci!*" Zoey replied as she adjusted the garment. "I think I need to take the waist in a bit, but that should be easy enough."

Zoey spent a few minutes pinning and then waited anxiously as Anne-Thérèse went to the changing room to carefully undress without getting hurt by the pins. Finally, Anne-Thérèse returned with the shorts and top and then left with the other models to get her hair and makeup done for the show. Zoey hurried to begin work on adjusting the shorts to fit her model perfectly. She'd lost some time helping Sean and then waiting for Anne-Thérèse to change, and didn't realize just *how* fast the hours before the show would really go. She wanted to look around and see how the other contestants were doing, but she didn't dare lift her head up from her own work.

The judging was held on another floor of the old building, which had been set up with a runway, folding chairs for the contestants and judges, and a small backstage area. Zoey was allowed to do some final primping on Anne-Thérèse, but then she had to go and sit in the audience to watch the show. She couldn't help feeling terrified. Her outfit, which had been hastily produced in less than a day, was about to walk down a real runway and be recorded for a real television show. It was so overwhelming, she decided to just push it out of her mind and enjoy watching everyone's outfits. After all, it wasn't often she got to attend a fashion show!

Once seated beside Sean, she noticed the judges file in. Two were from the regular show: Christophe

LeFrak and Aubrey Miller, both of whom Zoey had met when she was a guest judge on *Fashion Showdown*. The third was a designer named Solo.

When the production crew yelled *action*, Oscar stepped out onto the runway and introduced the show. The music came on, and the models began to walk.

Cat's outfit was an adorable jumpsuit, and Leanne's was a formal dress. A lot of contestants had sewn dresses, but one stood out to Zoey: A girl named Maude had made a retro dress out of the patterned fabric and added kick pleats that showed off the other fabric as the model walked.

Todd, the boy Sean had become friends with, had made flat-front shorts with a bandeau top from the bold fabric and layered them under a relaxed Hawaiian-style shirt made of the patterned fabric. Then Sean's model came out, wearing the one-shouldered top and slim pants with bold geometric stripes that he had made using the fabric salvaged from his first design. The pants looked like they fit a little better than the top, but his model had the best walk.

When it was Anne-Thérèse's turn to walk down the runway in Zoey's outfit, Zoey was proud. Her swingy top swung just right, and the high-waisted shorts were darling. Still, she was surprised to hear some oohs and aahs.

But as Anne-Thérèse turned to walk back, Zoey could see a flaw she was hoping wouldn't be noticeable. Zoey had had so little time to alter the shorts that the waist wasn't perfectly flat.

She knew she wouldn't get to hear the judges discussing her work in-depth until she saw the episode, because all the contestants waited backstage after the show while the judges talked. She decided that was probably for the best, in case they said anything really negative and the camera zoomed in on her for a reaction! It was going to be hard enough to keep her face calm when they announced the winner and who was going to be voted off.

The judges met together for more than an hour. In the green room, as the production team called it, the contestants were served food and drinks, and Zoey tried to relax and not worry. But she'd seen so many great designs; she had no idea where she'd be in the pack. At home, she was usually the best young fashion designer around, but here, she would have to really push herself to stand out. Zoey noticed Sean and Todd spending the whole break talking, but she just ate and absentmindedly flipped through a magazine.

At last, the contestants were called back into the runway area to hear the results. Oscar spoke a bit about the challenge and what a talented group of young designers they had. Sean reached over and squeezed Zoey's hand for good luck. She squeezed his hand back. One of the ten contestants was going to be voted off, and she hoped fervently it wouldn't be her or Sean.

Christophe spoke first. He announced the contestants who were in the middle of the pack, and therefore "safe." Sean, Leanne, Todd, and a girl named Pia were all safe. They each got up, joined their models on stage for a bow, and then walked out together. Zoey, Cat, and four others were left, either about to win or be in danger of being eliminated from the competition.

Zoey was thrilled Sean was safe, but she felt even more nervous that she was now sitting alone. She imagined her poor dad, having to watch this at home in a few days.

Zoey sat on her hands and bit her lip, trying not to look terrified. She didn't think Cat would be going home; everyone had liked her outfit.

The judges talked for a few minutes, discussing the remaining outfits. Zoey tried to listen carefully, but the words sounded like bees buzzing in her ear. They complimented Zoey's outfit, and its originality, but mentioned the ill-fitting waist several times and said she needed to take more time to finish the garment properly.

Finally, they announced that a boy named Martin, who'd made a sack dress that was too short on the model, was the one going home. Zoey couldn't help feeling sympathetic, as leaving first in front of everyone would be so hard. But he handled it well. He gave each contestant a hug and wished them luck and walked off the runway to go backstage.

Two others were declared safe, which left Zoey,

Cat, and Maude as potential winners. Zoey said a quick prayer that she wouldn't pass out on the stage in front of everyone.

Then Aubrey said, "The winner of this challenge, whose outfit showcases a delightful *joie de vivre*, as they say in Paris, is . . . Miss Zoey Webber."

Zoey felt all the blood rush to her head, and she felt so dizzy, she was worried she'd fall over. Cat nicely put a hand under her elbow to steady her. Zoey took a quick bow, remembering to thank the judges. She was shocked that in a room full of incredibly talented people, and in spite of the flaw in the shorts, she had won!

Oscar stepped forward to wrap up the show. When the cameras stopped rolling, the other contestants came back out, and everyone hurried to congratulate Zoey. Sean was beaming with pride, as if her win had made him almost as happy as if he'd won himself.

Then Rashida stepped forward and hushed everyone. "Great first show, team! I'm so impressed with the work you all did. We're sending this footage straight to editing, and it will run this week in the States. Now, we have tomorrow off, and then we travel to Milan the following morning. That means the rest of today and tomorrow is for sightseeing and fun! I've arranged a bunch of tours for you guys to sign up for, and remember, *you must be with a chaperone at all times*, unless you choose to stay in your suites. Understood?"

The group nodded obediently and then began talking, trying to decide what to do with their time off.

Sean turned to Zoey and gave her a huge hug. "You did it, Zoey! You won! It's so amazing. Let's celebrate. We'll go to the Louvre right now, and then the Musée d'Orsay and the Eiffel Tower tomorrow. We're in Paris, baby!"

Zoey's head spun. She wanted to call her dad immediately and tell him she'd won, but she wasn't allowed to tell anyone the news. She also wanted to collapse on the couch in her room for a while. But Sean was right. They were in Paris! And only for one and a half more days.

"Okay," she agreed. "Let's do it. But first, let's stop at one of those charming sidewalk cafés. I need a real meal, and I'm going to eat everything—maybe even the snails!"

Sean waggled his eyebrows. "Awesome! I've always wanted to try them."

"Oh?" Zoey said faintly. "Really? I was just kidding."

"Me too," he said, laughing. "I may be in Paris, but I'm *not* eating snails. Maybe I'm missing out, but I don't think I mind!"

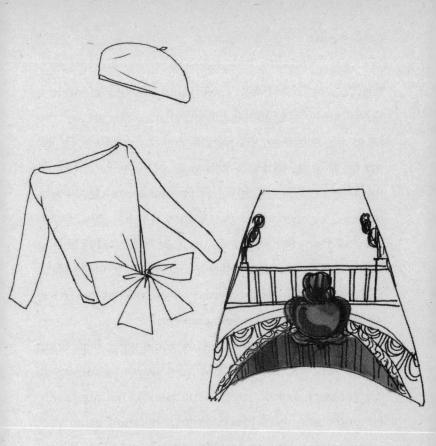

CHAPTER 8

J'adore Paris!

People aren't kidding when they say Paris is the most beautiful city in the world! *Fashion Showdown Junior* has been so awesome arranging tours for us, and S and I spent the last day and a half on buses and walking tours, zipping all around the city. We saw Montmartre, the Louvre, the Eiffel Tower, and walked along the Seine (the river that cuts through Paris). The art and the buildings and even the people are all gorgeous. I think my favorite thing that I saw was a Degas sculpture at the Musée d'Orsay called *Petite danseuse de 14 ans*, or *Small Dancer Aged 14*. I stared at it for ages. I wish we could stay in Paris longer, but we're actually packing right now to head to Milan! Luckily, it's a really short flight, and then—you guessed it—as soon as we arrive, we get to work on our next challenge!

I'm sure you're all *dying* to know what happened at the very first judging, but I am *sworn* to secrecy in my contract. I'm not even supposed to tell my family, although I can reveal that I was not eliminated, otherwise, I wouldn't be heading to Milan right now.☺ I can't even post sketches of what I'm making for the challenges. It's all top secret. Small price to pay, right?

This has truly been a magical trip so far, and my dad will not be happy to read this (sorry, Dad), but I haven't found a single second to do any of my schoolwork! Ack! I guess I'll save it all for the plane ride home from Italy, which someone told me is, like, nine hours. Maybe I can catch up then. However, I have learned a lot of new

French words, though, Dad, and that must count for something! *N'est-ce pas?*

Zoey didn't know quite what to expect in Italy, but it turned out to be very different from Paris. After a quick flight, the contestants were driven to their hotel to drop off their luggage. They were placed in a suite similar to the one in Paris, where everyone had their own room that connected to a common area. They were given a half hour or so to freshen up, and then they walked as a group to their new workroom.

Even during their short walk, Zoey was able to pick up the most common words, like *"ciao," "grazie,"* and *"prego."* She thought Milan seemed louder than Paris, with a different energy. People on scooters whizzed by them, going much faster on the cobblestone roads than Zoey thought possible, and the sidewalks were so narrow that they had to walk single file.

Zoey was in front, so she was the first to smell what turned out to be freshly baked semolina bread. As a treat, she bought them each a *cornetto*, a pastry similar to a croissant. It was a pretty great start to the day!

The new workroom was much like their previous one, which Zoey found comforting. She was also better rested than she'd been when she'd started the first project, which helped keep her nerves in check.

Once the cameras were rolling, Oscar began outlining the second challenge. "Contestants, welcome to Milan," he said, "one of the world's most fashionable cities. Italy is famous for its food, and especially for its pasta. Today, each of you will create a garment inspired by a shape of pasta."

The group murmured with surprise. Zoey grinned over at Sean, delighted to be doing something with an element of fun. An outfit based on a pasta shape was clearly an invitation to use her imagination and not focus quite as much on making a perfect garment, although she would definitely want to improve her finishing work this time!

"Just like last time, you'll have eight hours today to work and then a bit more time tomorrow morning to finish and make alterations. You will be using the same models, so measure accordingly. Good luck, or as they say in Italy, *'Buona fortuna!'*"

Each contestant was randomly assigned a pasta shape, and Zoey was given spaghetti. She had once made a spaghetti-themed dress for Kate, and she liked the idea of doing a new twist on the design. She quickly sketched a dress made with tubes of fabric in a variety of patterns looped around the model, like spaghetti swirled on a fork.

With only nine contestants remaining, everyone put their heads down and got to work. The day went by in a flash, as it had the first time, and while Zoey managed to get everything cut out and pinned, it wasn't all sewn together. She wondered if maybe her idea was too complicated, and she knew she would have to work very quickly the next morning to get the dress finished.

Zoey walked with Sean as the group headed back to their hotel. The streets were alive with people outside at tables on sidewalks, and others walking to and fro, chatting and laughing. Milan felt happy and busy. Zoey couldn't wait to get out and explore in another day or so.

"How's your project going?" Sean asked. He was making a dress inspired by bow-tie pasta, or farfalle, that cinched in the middle and flared out at the sides, just like a bow tie or a butterfly. He'd shown Zoey his sketch, and she thought it was a great idea.

"Ugh, mine's not so great at the moment," Zoey admitted. "I think I bit off more than I can chew. Get it?"

Sean laughed. "Ha! Well, at least you can make a joke. You know you'll pull it off in the end. . . . You always do!"

"How far along are you?" Zoey asked. "I love your design."

"Thanks," he said. "I feel like I'm getting warmed up now, and maybe have some idea what I'm doing. Before I came, I thought I had no chance of competing with all these people. But your advice, and seeing everyone else's runway outfits the other day, really inspired me."

Zoey smiled. She couldn't help noticing how much fun Sean seemed to be having on the trip. He was much more social than she was with the other contestants too—hanging out with them in the common room at night and sitting with them at lunch. He seemed to feel at home with everybody. Zoey liked everyone too, particularly Cat and Leanne, but she felt like having Sean along was all she really needed for support. She didn't feel as motivated to make friends, probably because there was so much to do for each challenge, and she had Kate, Libby, and Priti e-mailing her day and night to check in.

"You're so talented, Sean," she told him. "I think you have a real shot at winning with your bow-tie dress."

Sean frowned. "Maybe. We'll see. I've got a lot to do tomorrow. I think tonight I'll go straight to bed instead of hanging out."

"Me too," said Zoey. "What's Italian for 'good night' again? Oh yeah—*buona notte*."

"*Buona notte*," Sean replied with a grin.

The next morning was a frantic blur. Glad to have her model's measurements already, Zoey sewed furiously, trying to make her dress look as finished as possible. She didn't even have time to check out anyone else's designs. She was actually looking forward to watching the shows when they aired, so she could see everyone else working and how they went about it. There was never time in the workroom for her to notice anything! She occasionally helped Sean, and he occasionally helped her, but that was it.

After Anne-Thérèse came in for her fitting, Zoey was relieved to see the garment's length was fine, and the dress just needed a few seams taken in. She got to work, smoothing and tweaking different parts of the dress, trying to make the fit as perfect as possible. She liked her spaghetti concept, and how she'd represented it with the mix of different fabrics, but she wasn't sure the cut of the dress was her best. With only about ten or eleven hours total to create an outfit from scratch, and a lot of pressure, she thought maybe it just wasn't possible to make something perfect.

After the models were dressed, Zoey and the rest of the group headed to their new makeshift runway and judging area. It was as cold as the workroom in Paris had been. Luckily, Zoey had done some shopping in Paris. In addition to buying gifts for her family and friends, she'd bought herself a lovely pashmina, which she tied artfully around herself, knotting it by her hip.

One by one, the models came down the runway. Sean's bow-tie dress looked great, and he'd used a beautiful fuchsia fabric that really stood out. Maude had made a campanelle-inspired dress. Zoey had never seen *campanelle* before, but it was kind of like a trumpet shape with a ruffled edge. It was a beautiful shape, and Maude had designed a gown with layers of chiffon that formed the fluted skirt. Then it was time for Cat's penne dress, a futuristic-looking tube with the hem and neckline cut at an angle. It was one of Zoey's favorites. In fact, Zoey liked most of the designs better than her own, and she started to doubt herself.

When the runway show had finished, the group was dismissed to the green room to wait while the judges talked over everything.

"I like your spaghetti dress," Cat said to Zoey as they stood at the refreshments table, with Cat picking at a muffin and Zoey making tea. "You have a great eye for mixing prints."

"Thanks," Zoey said gratefully. "But I don't like mine half as much as your penne dress. It's gorgeous and so sleek!"

The group chatted and snacked and took turns anxiously checking the light on the wall, which would glow green when it was time for them to go back out to the judging area. The wait seemed to be much longer than it had been the first time, and Zoey started to feel like she was the one going home. She didn't know why, but she had a very bad feeling.

At last, they were called back. The judges thanked them for their hard work and then announced several names that were safe. They didn't call Sean or Zoey. That meant they were either in the top or bottom. The five who hadn't been named as safe were asked to come stand on stage, beside their models. Zoey felt like she wobbled a bit as she walked up the steps.

When she took her place alongside Anne-Thérèse, the model quickly grabbed Zoey's hand

and gave it a reassuring squeeze. "Don't worry," she whispered. "This dress is beautiful!"

The judges began assessing each individual outfit. Zoey hoped she wouldn't faint.

"Miss Webber?" Aubrey said. "Tell us about your dress."

Zoey cleared her throat, hoping her voice wouldn't come out as a squeak. "Well, I've always loved spaghetti, and, um, angel hair and linguine." Zoey paused, realizing what she was saying had nothing to do with her design. "So, um, anyway, I like how spaghetti swirls around a fork and used that as the basis for this dress, but with contrasting prints to give the noodle shapes some impact."

Zoey coughed, praying she wasn't coming across as terrified and incoherent on camera as she felt in real life.

Solo said, "Well, Zoey, I like that you used different fabrics; it tells me a lot about your point of view. And I love the fabrics you chose. They show that you have a wonderful sense of color. However, the cut of the dress . . . it just isn't very flattering."

Zoey held her breath and set her mouth in a

hard line, trying to appear calm and attentive.

Then it was Christophe's turn. "I agree—not a flattering cut at all, even on a model! I wonder if maybe using the fabrics vertically would have been better?" He looked at his co-judges, and they nodded in agreement.

"Yes, yes, I think that's right," Aubrey said. "They would have stayed flatter and looked more intentional instead of like a bit of a mess."

Zoey felt her heart sink. A mess? This could be it. Her final moment on *Fashion Showdown Junior*. Based on these comments, she was clearly one of the bottom two or three, and not one of the potential winners.

Thankfully, the judges moved on then, to Maude and then Sean, whose outfits they loved.

Zoey bit her lip and clenched and unclenched her hands, trying to tell herself no matter what happened, she'd smile and thank the judges and walk off with her head held high. Her family and friends would still be proud of her. She'd gotten to travel to France and Italy, and that was pretty amazing.

As the judges got ready to make their

announcement, Zoey breathed in and out several times. It would be over in a minute.

"And the person who will be leaving us today is . . . Todd."

Zoey felt so lightheaded with relief at not being cut from the show, she worried she'd float right up to the ceiling. At the same time, she felt bad for Todd. He seemed really nice and had been friendly with Sean. But she was glad to be able to go to the next challenge and the next country! Not to mention, she'd be able to show her face at school next week, knowing she hadn't been voted off yet.

Zoey looked at Sean. She could see he was tense as well, though from the comments he'd gotten, she felt sure he was in contention for winning.

"And the winner of this challenge is . . . ," said Solo, "Maude, with the beautiful campanelle ball gown. Congratulations, Maude."

As Oscar and the judges took some final shots, Zoey and Sean and the rest of the contestants started to collect their belongings to head back to the hotel.

Sean walked over to Zoey and said, "Ready for

some sightseeing? Milan is waiting for us!"

Zoey couldn't believe how buoyant Sean looked. But then again, he'd almost won and she'd almost been sent home. Zoey groaned, feeling thoroughly wrung out. "I need a hot shower first. That was terrifying!"

Sean nodded. "Totally. I had no idea how stressful the judging would be. It looks bad on TV, but it's *way* worse in real life. Are we sure we know what we're doing?"

Zoey snorted. "*You* almost won, Sean! You definitely know what you're doing."

"And *you* already won one," he reminded her. "You just need to be less ambitious next time and remember your time limit."

"Maybe," she agreed. Sean was right. She *had* won one challenge. Maybe that helped save her today. "Spaghetti might make me feel better."

"Make mine bow-tie pasta," he said. "And then let's go see the Duomo di Milano and that convent where Da Vinci's *The Last Supper* is. After all, it is our *last supper* in Italy!"

"Ha-ha," Zoey said. "Very funny."

CHAPTER 9

Arrivederci, Milan!

You guys, Italy is amazing. I wish we had time to visit a few other cities, because I can't get enough of everything Italian! I've seen so many beautiful churches, museums, sculptures, paintings, gardens, and bowls of spaghetti carbonara. (My new favorite food—it has egg in it, so it's kind of like breakfast on top of pasta!) Although the best thing I've eaten by far is gelato, which is Italian ice cream, only it's so much better than regular ice cream!

We're heading to the airport soon to fly home, and I am SO EXCITED to see my family and friends! I missed them every minute. I have gifts for everyone, but of course I didn't leave myself enough room in my suitcase, so I had to cram it all in and then ask two other contestants to come in and sit on my suitcase so I could zip it. I still can't tell you anything about the results of the second show, which is so, so hard. It airs next week, I think, and I'll be able to watch it in my own living room. I'm curious to see how frantic and nutty I look on camera.☺ I've never sewed so hard and fast in my life! Please, when you watch the show, remind yourself how little time we had to make these creations and that every one of these awesome designers worked their bottoms off to get their garment made in time!

And to my besties whom I have missed so much . . . I'm coming home, girls! Order a pizza and make room on the couch!

Walking down the hallway at school on Monday was surreal. Zoey felt like she'd been gone for so long, and at the same time, it was like she'd never left! But one thing had changed for sure. Up and down the hallway, kids were waving to her or yelling things like, "Way to go, Zoey!" Some of them were wearing layered outfits similar to what Zoey had worn in the cold workroom in Paris. She didn't know what to make of all the attention, and simply waved back at kids who spoke to her and continued moving swiftly toward her locker.

She hadn't had a chance to see her friends over the weekend, since she'd arrived back so late on Saturday, and her dad had insisted she spend Sunday catching up on sleep and homework. Ms. Austen had come over for dinner that night, and Zoey had given her the scarf she'd bought her in Paris. But she had gifts for her friends as well, and she couldn't wait to hand them out.

As Zoey approached her locker, she saw Priti, Libby, and Kate—as well as a large sign that read FASHION SHOWDOWN JUNIOR STAR! They cheered, and Priti launched herself toward Zoey, arms outstretched. The four of them ended up in a group hug.

"We *missed* you, Zoey!" said Libby.

"So much," Kate agreed. "School felt empty without you. And we watched the Paris episode together, and saw you win, and we couldn't even congratulate you in person!"

"I can't believe you WON, Zoey!" Priti squealed. "You're going to win the whole thing! I know it!"

Zoey beamed. "Thanks, but I probably won't. Everyone is *so* talented, you guys. It's amazing. I finally understand the saying 'a little fish in a big pond.'"

"You're a big fish no matter where you go," Libby insisted. "Ezra's good-luck charm must have brought you extra-special luck!"

Zoey slapped her forehead. Her phone had buzzed with a message from Ezra that morning, but she'd forgotten to read it because she'd been packing up for school and hurrying to get out the door. "Yikes! I got text from him earlier. Lemme check it. . . ."

Hey, fashion superstar! Will u be too busy with

reporters this week to come over and watch a movie or play some video games?

Zoey read it aloud to her friends. Libby oohed and aahed. "Write back!" she said. "Tell him you'd love to!"

Zoey hesitated. It seemed harsh, but she'd hardly thought about Ezra while she'd been gone—even with his good-luck charm on her bracelet! And while she appreciated his company, she had school-work to catch up on, and she wanted to spend time with her besties, her dad, Marcus, and Aunt Lulu and Uncle John. She wasn't sure she was willing to sacrifice any of her time with them to see Ezra, especially when she'd be off to Japan in less than two weeks.

Zoey glanced at Kate, who again seemed to understand without a word what Zoey was thinking.

"Maybe answer him later?" Kate suggested. "It's hard for you to think when we're all standing here staring at you."

Zoey slid her phone into her pocket. "Good idea," she said. "I'm going to send him a text and explain how crazy things are, and hopefully, he'll understand. But right now I want to give you guys your gifts, because the bell's going to ring any minute!"

She unzipped her bag and pulled out three small packages.

Priti, looking pleased, unwrapped hers the fastest. "Oh, Zoey," she said as she pulled out a bracelet with a tiny Eiffel Tower charm on it. "I love it!"

"Me too!" cried Libby, examining hers. "I've always wanted to go to Paris, and now I can pretend I have!"

The girls put on their bracelets, and Zoey held up her wrist. Her own charm bracelet had a newly added Eiffel Tower charm.

"*Très chic,*" Priti said, giggling at her own joke.

Zoey and Kate chuckled too, but Libby was all business. "So, Zoey," she began, "we're dying to know what happened in Milan! Did you win? We won't tell, promise!"

Zoey sighed. "I'd love to tell you everything, but they made me sign something promising I wouldn't. All I can say is that since Sean and I are going to Japan, you can tell that we didn't get voted off."

Libby smiled. "That's something! Cool!"

The bell rang, and the girls began to walk down the hallway together toward their homerooms. Kids continued to congratulate Zoey, who couldn't help thinking that as soon as the Milan episode aired in a few days, they'd be less enthusiastic.

Noticing her silence, Priti asked, "Is it good to be home, Zoey? Or are you sad?"

"It's not good to be home," said Zoey. "It's great."

At lunch Zoey sat with her friends, still reveling in the normalcy of being at school. She enjoyed her grilled cheese sandwich and fries, as well as the noise of the crowded cafeteria. She especially enjoyed not being on camera. She hadn't realized how tense she'd been during the filming.

As the girls were catching up on gossip, Gabe appeared and plopped down next to Zoey.

"Hey, Zo! Congrats on the Paris challenge. How does it feel to be an international star?"

Zoey laughed. She definitely didn't feel like an international star after the Milan challenge. "I got lucky with a good idea," she said.

"It was more than luck," Gabe insisted, his brown eyes sincere. "And I still want to capture your rise to fame for the school newspaper. They want me to include an article now too. Can I ask you a few questions?"

Zoey felt both flattered and overwhelmed by the idea, but she agreed.

"Okay," she said gamely. "I can't reveal results, but I can tell you about all the amazing food I ate and shopping I did. Oh, and the cathedrals. There were so many cathedrals!"

As Gabe wrote down some notes and took a few pictures, Zoey felt more relaxed. It was more like a conversation than an interview, and Gabe fit right in with her group of friends, almost like he'd always been a part of it.

After school Zoey sat cross-legged on her couch, doing homework. She couldn't believe how hard it was to make up a week of school. With a sigh, she put her papers down and got up to make a snack.

On her way to the kitchen, she noticed a new picture on the mantel in front of the Webber family photo from when Zoey was a baby. It was of her dad and Ms. Austen, holding hands at the beach. The Webbers lived more than an hour from the coast, and Zoey hadn't realized they had gone to the shore together. It felt like she was seeing some secret part of their relationship that her dad had never mentioned to her.

Scowling, she continued into the kitchen. On the fridge, she found another picture of the happy couple, this one in a plastic magnetic frame. They were at the stadium at the university where her father worked. Part of her dad's job was to be on call during sporting events, and it made sense that Ms. Austen would attend some of the games, but Zoey hadn't really thought about it before. Zoey wondered suddenly just how much time they spent together.

As she opened the fridge to hunt for leftovers, Marcus walked in. "Hey, Zo!" he said. "I'd almost forgotten what it was like to have you home."

"Ha-ha," she said. "I'd almost forgotten how *not* funny you are."

"Oooh, someone's prickly," he replied, joining

her in the front of the fridge. "What's eating you? Get it?"

Zoey usually loved her brother's jokes, but today she wasn't in the mood. "While I was gone, Dad put out all these pictures of him and Ms. Austen. And they're so . . . so, well, *personal*."

She shut the fridge door, so he could see the plastic frame on the front.

Marcus eyed the photo curiously. "Personal? They're at a soccer game. In a stadium."

Zoey groaned. "Never mind."

"No, not never mind. Talk."

Zoey tried to find the words to explain how she felt. "It's just . . . she was here for dinner last night when I'd just gotten home, and she's hanging around dad's work, apparently, and now photos of her and dad are all over the house. It's like she's trying to replace Mom or something."

Marcus looked thoughtful. "Well, Mom and Essie do have a lot in common, you know."

"No, they don't!" Zoey snapped. "Mom was amazing and unique and creative."

Marcus grabbed the peanut butter and bread and

moved to the counter to make a sandwich. "Yeah, she was. And Essie is too, and she cares about Dad and us a lot. She's not so bad, you know."

"I *know*, Marcus. I knew her first! She's *my* principal!" Zoey turned without getting a snack and stormed off back into the living room to her pile of work. She'd lost her appetite.

"I think you're just cranky because you're seriously jet-lagged, Zoey. Maybe you need a nap!" Marcus yelled after her.

Zoey flopped down on the couch, too irritable to study. She picked up the remote and turned on the TV. Maybe Marcus was right. But while she'd been away, it was like Ms. Austen had taken the opportunity to practically move right in.

A little while later Zoey heard her father's car in the driveway. When he walked in alone, Zoey sighed with relief. She wanted to have dinner with just him and Marcus that night.

As her dad began chopping chicken and vegetables to make a stir-fry, Zoey wandered into the kitchen. "Can I help?" she asked.

Mr. Webber smiled. "Music to my ears. Set the table, please, and pour some water."

Zoey got out three place settings.

"Four places, Zoey," he said, correcting her. "Essie'll be here any minute."

Zoey's stomach lurched. Before she could protest, she heard a double-knock, and then the front door opening. "Hello, Webbers!" Ms. Austen called.

Zoey barely had time to take a breath and wipe the frown from her face before Ms. Austen was in the kitchen.

"Hi, Zoey!" she said. "I can't tell you how many compliments I got on this scarf today. Thank you so much! You know my taste exactly."

"I'm glad you like it," replied Zoey, somewhat listlessly. She started to fold the napkins into little shapes, to keep her hands busy.

"Everyone at school was talking about you today," Ms. Austen went on. "The teachers, the students—everyone."

Mr. Webber nodded. "People at work keep telling me they saw you win, Zo, and I get to say, 'Yep, that's my daughter!' We're so proud of you, honey."

"Thank you," Zoey said automatically, still thinking about how when her dad said "we're," he had put his arm around Ms. Austen.

"Now that you're back, Zoey," Ms. Austen said as she helped Zoey's dad dole out stir-fry, "I'd love to have a girls' outing so I can hear more about your trip. I went to Europe when I was in college, and it was the best time of my life! Maybe we could go shopping or to tea? Or I could take you to the fabric store? I'd love to see where you get the materials to work your magic."

Zoey was silent for a moment, unsure of how to answer. It wasn't that she didn't like Ms. Austen or shopping or tea. It was just . . . annoying. Not only was Ms. Austen there all the time, but even when she *wasn't* there, her picture was on the fridge and on the mantel, and Zoey wanted a break. Plus, she really didn't want to be seen in public with the school principal. Even if people didn't figure out that it meant Ms. Austen and Zoey's dad were dating, they'd probably start calling Zoey the principal's pet. And she had enough to worry about with the next challenge around the corner.

"Um, I think I'm going to have to stay really focused on schoolwork this week," Zoey said. After a second she added, "But thanks."

Her father looked at her sharply, and then he called, "Marcus! Dinner!"

They all sat down, and Zoey tried to be pleasant while they ate. She knew her father wasn't happy she'd turned down Ms. Austen's invitation.

Luckily, Marcus was unusually chatty, talking about a gig he'd lined up for his band and a potential summer job he'd gotten as a music counselor at a camp nearby.

Zoey noticed Ms. Austen watching her during the meal, and she did her best to act normally. But inside, she was counting the seconds until she could run up to her room and hide.

Later, as Zoey was sitting on her bed, finishing up yet another page of math problems, there was a knock on her door.

"Come in," she called, hoping it was Marcus.

It was her father, looking rather uneasy.

"What's up?" she asked.

"You tell me," he said, sitting down on her bed. "I know you just had the trip of a lifetime, and you're a big TV star now, but can you please explain why you were so rude to Essie this evening? She's gone home, by the way, so speak freely."

Zoey sighed. Her dad had it all wrong. "It's not about being a star, or whatever, Dad," she said. "I'd just like to have dinner alone with you and Marcus for once. Didn't you guys see each other enough while I was gone? I see Ms. Austen at school *every day*, and in our kitchen almost every night, too! I need some space, that's all. And what if someone catches on when they see us together?"

Her dad was quiet. He didn't look angry or even hurt. Just thoughtful. "You know," he said after a minute. "Me dating someone special is still very new for you and Marcus. And I get that it's difficult, especially for you, since you knew Essie before this. I thought it might be easier since you seemed to get along so well with her at school, but it's normal for there to be some growing pains."

Zoey couldn't help cracking a small smile. "'Growing pains'?"

"Well, that's what we called it in my day," he said. "Now people call it 'being a teenager.' On top of all this, you're just on the cusp of a lot of changes in your life, and I think you're going to be glad to have Essie around, once you get used to the idea. But you need to give her a chance, Zoey."

Zoey wanted to say that it had *nothing* to do with her becoming a teenager, but held back. "She's trying to be my best friend, Dad. It's weird."

"She's not, Zoey. She's just trying to figure out how to be part of your life outside of school. You guys are actually so similar—'cut from the same cloth,' as they say. If you can take a step back, I think you'd remember that."

Zoey thought about how much she used to enjoy going to Ms. Austen's office to talk about her blog and her Etsy site. And how she'd always admired Ms. Austen's fashion sense and how it was Ms. Austen who had abolished uniforms at Mapleton Prep, which had really kick-started Zoey's interest in sewing.

"I could try a little harder," Zoey admitted. "But I'm not quite ready for us to be a family, okay?"

"I understand, Zo," said her dad. "And, please, don't feel like you can't talk to me about all this. No matter what, *you* will always be my number-one girl, okay?"

"Okay," she said, letting her dad wrap her in his arms.

After her father left, she picked up her sketchbook instead of her math sheet. She was still frustrated by the Ms. Austen invasion, but at least her dad seemed to get it. Zoey wasn't sure being a teenager had anything to do with it, but for some reason, that made her feel like less of a jerk.

CHAPTER 10

Home Again, Home Again

Remember that nursery rhyme, "To market, to market to buy a fat pig? Home again, home again" and so on? Well, I'm enjoying being home (except for the homework), and I'm also trying to help my aunt get ready for her soon-to-be-born baby by making this receiving outfit with a nursery-rhyme fabric!

Anyway, I've been sketching a lot since I've been home, but I haven't sewn any outfits other than this one. My fingers still feel cramped up from sewing for the Milan challenge! It's going to air in two days, and I'm nerrrrrrvous to watch myself, because I know how much I was sweating to get everything done!

I'm off to visit my aunt and her baby bump today, and I can't wait to see how much bigger she's gotten! (Sorry, Aunt L! I mean that in the nicest way!) Is there anything harder than waiting for a baby to be born? Especially a little cousin you've wanted forever?

Saturday morning, Marcus dropped Zoey off at their aunt's house. When Zoey knocked, she was surprised to hear a faint "Come in!" from somewhere inside the house instead of having her aunt answering the door.

"Aunt Lulu?" Zoey called, opening the door and stepping inside. Buttons, Lulu's dog, came running up enthusiastically, covering Zoey with doggie kisses. "Where are you?"

"The kitchen," Lulu replied.

Zoey found Lulu sitting in a straight-backed kitchen chair, sipping a large glass of water with lemon.

"Are you okay?" Zoey asked, concerned. Lulu looked not just pregnant but puffy. Her face, her hands, and her massive belly, all made her look like a hot-air balloon version of herself.

"Perfectly fine," Lulu answered, smiling. "Just very pregnant. I can't sit on the sofa, because I sink down and can't get back up, and hurrying to answer the door is not an option. And I'm keeping my feet propped up to help my swollen ankles. So things are a bit more casual around here now."

Zoey laughed, glad to see that Aunt Lulu's sense of humor was exactly the same as it had always been.

"I made some coffee cake for us. How about you slice it up, get us some iced tea, and tell me *every last thing* about your trip, all right?"

Zoey agreed, happy to wait on them and let Lulu sit. Once they had their treats, Zoey launched into a play-by-play of her time in France and Italy, and Lulu listened, spellbound.

"Can't you just tell me the results from Milan, Zoey?"

Zoey shook her head. "I can't tell *anyone!*"

"Well, I'm impressed that you can keep it a secret! I'm not sure I could."

"I'd better change the subject so I don't crack!" Zoey said. "I'm working on a receiving outfit for the baby, to give you before I leave for Japan."

"Oh, Zoey!" said Lulu. "I can't wait for the baby to wear it."

Buttons licked Zoey's leg, and she scratched her behind her ears. "Is Buttons getting excited?" Zoey asked.

"Hard to say, but she definitely senses some changes around here," Aunt Lulu said, patting her round stomach. Zoey must have looked pensive because Aunt Lulu quickly said, "Zoey, what is it?"

"Oh, well, uh . . ." Zoey couldn't quite get the words out. Looking at Lulu's belly, she'd just now realized that if her dad and Ms. Austen really did get *serious* serious, they might decide to have a baby too. And Zoey would have another sibling. And Ms. Austen would be its mother.

"Talk to me," Lulu said.

Zoey wanted to tell her everything, but Lulu looked so tired and stressed, and Zoey didn't want to unload on her.

"I'm fine, Aunt Lulu," she said. "There's just a lot going on with school and getting ready to leave again. I've been trying to spend time with my friends, and lately, Ms. Austen wants to hang out with me too. . . ."

Lulu smiled slightly, as if she'd known all along that that was where the conversation was headed. "It's okay, Zoey. Your dad told me what's going on."

Relieved, Zoey spilled her guts. "It feels like she's trying to take Mom's place."

"She's not," Lulu said definitively. "And she never could. Essie will bring new and different things to your family, and you should try to be open to them. But she will not ever try to be your mom. She will be herself."

"Really?" said Zoey.

"*Really,*" Lulu assured her.

Feeling much better, Zoey had a second piece of coffee cake before realizing she needed to leave to meet Kate and Libby at the movies. "Can I peek into the nursery before I go?" she asked Lulu. "I love looking at it."

"Of course! Please excuse me if I don't get up . . . ," she joked.

Zoey laughed and then headed down the hallway into the peaceful nursery. She knew it wouldn't be long now until she'd be helping Lulu rock the baby to sleep in the glider.

The next week at school flew by. Zoey visited her favorite store, A Stitch in Time, and got the royal treatment from Jan, the owner. The Milan challenge aired, and Zoey invited her friends over to watch it, even though she was nervous about how she'd come across on TV. To her surprise, she mostly appeared very focused and not nearly as panicked as she'd felt on the inside. She could tell by the way the show was edited that they were depicting her as the "serious" contestant. While some of the others, including Sean, were often filmed laughing and having fun, she was always shown working with her head down. She decided that was okay with her, since she was less likely to embarrass herself that way!

Zoey expected kids at school to give her some grief over losing the challenge and getting such harsh feedback on her spaghetti dress. But instead, she found they were mostly supportive, telling her they'd liked the dress and that it had seemed like a particularly hard challenge for everyone. Even Ivy, who until recently had hardly said a nice word to Zoey since they started together at Mapleton Prep, made a point of telling her the judges had been "really harsh."

Zoey appreciated everyone's support more than she could say. Priti said everyone had been envious when they'd first heard Zoey was going to be on TV, but once they'd seen how tough the competition was, they'd realized it wasn't all fun. It was hard, hard work. Zoey tried to be gracious and humble, and she made a point to turn most conversations quickly back to schoolwork, to show she hadn't changed and was still a normal middle schooler. Trying to be normal was hard work too.

That Saturday, Zoey was packed and ready to leave for Japan. She'd had a few long talks with Ezra over the past week and made it clear to him that she had decided she wanted to be friends only. While he seemed slightly disappointed, he'd remained friendly and had already texted a good-luck message for her next challenge.

Gabe was coming over to document her final preparations for his photo essay. Zoey had asked her father, nicely, that Ms. Austen not come by so things wouldn't be weird or fishy at school. Even though she trusted Gabe to keep things a secret, she didn't want him to know the story yet. Her father agreed and didn't even say anything about growing pains. When Zoey had said good-bye to Ms. Austen the day before, she had tried to be open like Aunt Lulu had suggested, and it helped.

Sean was at the house too, since Mr. Webber had offered to drive him to the airport since his parents couldn't leave work early that day.

"I'm glad you're here," Gabe told Sean, and asked if he could take pictures of him too, since he was on the show as well. Sean agreed, and Gabe took photos of them reviewing the prep lists the production team had sent them for Japan and China. Then Gabe interviewed them both, asking what they were most nervous and most excited about.

It was a fun morning, and Zoey was less nervous about the next challenge than she thought she'd be. Something about having Gabe there put her at ease. It also probably helped that kids at school had been nicer than expected about her losing the Milan challenge. Suddenly, some of the pressure was off.

Zoey looked at the clock and noticed it was almost time to leave for the airport.

As Gabe was packing up his camera and getting ready to leave, Mr. Webber came running out of the house, his face red and his eyes wide. "Zoey! Lulu might be in early labor, and Uncle John's away on a business trip. I've got to take her to the hospital and help until John can get here. And Marcus is at SAT prep class, so he's not answering his phone, and neither are Sean's parents. I had to call Essie—I mean, Ms. Austen—to take you guys to the airport, okay? She's on her way."

Zoey heard her dad slip Ms. Austen's first name

but didn't care—she only wanted to know if Aunt Lulu and the baby would be all right. "Dad, are they going to be okay? Forget the trip, I need to go to the hospital with you!"

Her father shook his head. "No, Zoey, your aunt would never want you to miss this trip. Besides, she might not have the baby for a few more days, or even weeks, if it's a false alarm."

"But what if it's while I'm *away*?" Zoey asked, on the verge of crying. She did *not* want to miss her cousin's birth. Not even for *Fashion Showdown Junior*.

"I promise I'll send you updates," her father said as she, Gabe, and Sean followed him to his car. "This is nonnegotiable, sweetie. Even if she's born today, the baby will still be brand-new when you get home. I'm sorry, but I *have* to go."

He opened the garage door just as Ms. Austen pulled up in her car. "I'm here! I drove as fast I could. Sean, Zoey, are you guys all set? Oh, hi, Gabe!"

Zoey finally remembered Gabe and Sean were still standing there. They were staring at Ms. Austen and looking confused.

"Um, hi, Ms. Austen," Gabe said.

"Hi, Ms. Austen," Sean echoed him.

Ms. Austen glanced at Zoey, whose face was turning beet red. "Principals are ready to help with any crisis," she said, trying to act natural. "Time to get two of my most talented students off to the airport."

Exhaling, Zoey said, "Oh forget it. Sean, Gabe . . . my dad and Ms. Austen are dating. Like, dating *seriously*. And you can't tell anyone at school, okay?"

Gabe nodded. "Whatever you want . . . but, I mean, that's great!"

"I can't believe you didn't tell me, Zo!" Sean added. Then he cracked a wicked grin. "But go, Mr. Webber!"

Now Mr. Webber's cheeks turned red. But he was rushing to leave, so he gave Zoey a swift hug and said, "Good luck, Zoey. *Don't worry*—Lulu's just fine. You focus on you!"

"I'll try," whispered Zoey.

He turned to Ms. Austen. "Thanks again, Essie. Get my girl off safely, okay?" She nodded, and he kissed her on the cheek.

Zoey noticed Gabe's eyes bug out. With her mind occupied by thoughts of Aunt Lulu and the baby, Zoey didn't even worry about the fact that the secret was out.

Gabe asked if he could take a few quick photos of Sean and Zoey walking to the car, promising not to include Ms. Austen. When he was done, Zoey and Sean climbed into Ms. Austen's car, waved good-bye to Gabe, and were off. After the adventure of the last few minutes, going to Japan and China seemed like no big deal.

CHAPTER 11

Sushi Style!

Konnichiwa! That's Japanese for "good day," and it's all I know of the language so far. I'm thrilled to be in Japan, but honestly, all I'm doing is checking my phone and worrying about my aunt, who we thought went into early labor just as I was leaving. It was just a false alarm, but the baby still could arrive any day! Now I'm headed to our challenge, and I just don't know how I'll concentrate!

The group is smaller now, with just eight contestants, so I feel even more pressure. Someone will go home tomorrow. I studied the Japanese version of *Très Chic* that my aunt gave me for the plane, as a going-away present, hoping to inspire myself with beautiful Japanese fashion! Wish me luck. I'm really going to need it this time! The competition is fierce!

Aside from the hotel being more modern than those in France and Italy, Zoey had a sense of déjà vu from the first trip. She saw a bit of Tokyo on the way to the workroom. The city was crowded and dense, with incredibly tall buildings, neon billboards, and people everywhere. Seeing Japanese characters on everything instead of her own English alphabet was both bizarre and wonderful, and Zoey was immediately inspired by the beautiful shapes of the kanji.

While the production crew set up everything for the challenge, Sean and the other contestants chatted and compared photos of Tokyo, but Zoey kept checking her phone.

The camera crew approached her and asked if she was worried about her aunt.

"How did you . . . ," Zoey began but then realized something. "Of course. You read my blog post."

She wished she had remembered to think twice before posting her innermost thoughts for the world—and *Fashion Showdown Junior* staff—to see!

Finally, Oscar appeared, and thankfully, all eyes were on him. He announced their third challenge. They would have eight hours to create a modern interpretation of a kimono.

Zoey immediately got to work, intending to make hers a pantsuit with a loose kimono-style jacket.

Several hours into the challenge, as she was beginning to baste the pants, her phone buzzed. Zoey grabbed it and saw a picture of a red-faced newborn.

Baby Melissa, read the text from her dad. **Happy, healthy, and perfect!**

Baby Melissa, after Zoey's mom and Aunt Lulu's sister! What an amazing thing for Lulu and Uncle John to do. Zoey felt a moment of intense relief and joy, and then without warning, her eyes welled up, and hot tears poured down her cheeks. She realized just how much she missed her mother and how unfair it was that she couldn't meet her namesake. It felt even worse than it did when she was little because now that she was becoming a teenager and dealing with more grown-up things, she needed her mother to talk to.

Then something occurred to her. What if maybe Ms. Austen could one day feel like a mother to her? For some reason, having the baby named Melissa made Zoey feel like there would be less of a chance now of anyone erasing her mother's memory. Her mother's name would be alive and well in their family, and in a way, so would her mother's spirit. Ms. Austen could just be one *more* person in the family. Not a replacement . . . but an addition. The realization shed a very different light on things.

Sean came over and handed Zoey a tissue. "Cute!" he said when he saw the photo of the new baby. "But don't you dare give up on this contest, Zoey," he whispered. "The countdown is still on, and if you stay focused, you've got a real chance here."

Zoey wiped at her eyes, but concentrating on the challenge seemed impossible. Yes, this was the opportunity of a lifetime, but all she wanted to do was go home and hold Baby Melissa—the newest member of her family—in her arms.

The cameras zoomed in on Zoey and Sean, and Oscar came over and asked, "Zoey, are you okay? Is there news?"

Zoey smiled. "I have a new cousin," she said softly, deciding this moment was too special, too private, to share more of her feelings with the world. "And a challenge to focus on!"

"Give her some room?" Sean said, waving the cameras away, and then he patted Zoey on the back. "Just a few more hours, okay? You've got this."

Their time in Tokyo flew by. Zoey's kimono-style jacket turned out fairly well, considering, and she ended up in the safe group. Sean made the top two again, although he didn't win. The winner was Cat, with a kimono-inspired romper. A girl named Sally, who had always been in the middle of the pack, was sent home. There was only one competition left. Six of the seven remaining contestants would be having a runway show of their own, but one would be cut. As the group visited the Tokyo Tower and the Tsujiki Market, Zoey hoped Sean and Leanne would do well in Shanghai.

When the plane landed in Shanghai, Zoey forgot all about the competition when her phone buzzed with a new picture of her baby cousin. But she resolved not to lose focus on the final challenge, which was to represent with their garments one thing China is famous for.

Zoey was inspired by the Great Wall of China and made a sleek, green shift dress with tan-colored zippers to mimic the shape of the wall when seen from above. She'd spent so many hours putting in zippers that these lay perfectly flat.

Sean represented China's famous giant pandas with a black-and-white evening gown, with shoulders that mimicked panda ears.

In the final judging, the judges gushed about Zoey's dress, giving it one compliment after another.

Zoey, Leanne, and Sean all landed in the top group, but in the end, it was Sean who won the challenge. A girl named Drea went home. Zoey thought it must have been especially hard to get so close but not make it. In the end, Zoey, Sean, Leanne, Maude, Cat, and Pia would go to New York for the runway finale. Win or lose, she was also relieved that she could finally, *finally* go home to meet her new cousin.

On the plane ride home, Zoey sat with Sean, both of them tired, but far too wired from all the adrenaline to fall asleep.

"You know, Zo, I couldn't have won without you," Sean said, nudging her with his elbow. "I would have been sent home after the very first challenge!"

"You would have not," said Zoey. "And you got better with every single challenge! That's the way to do it, unlike me, who started strong and fell apart."

"You had a lot going on," he said. "And we're

both still in it, which means we get to go home and work *really hard* for the next few weeks, to bring two new looks to add to our collections for the runway finale. Have you thought about what you'll make?"

Zoey shook her head. She couldn't think of anything beyond seeing everyone she loved. Zoey's dad had told her that Lulu and the baby were both doing well and were at home from the hospital, and they could drive there straight from the airport if Aunt Lulu and Uncle John were up for visitors.

Zoey had enjoyed traveling, but a part of her never wanted to leave her family again. She wondered how she would ever go away to college one day—maybe to fashion design school in New York City—if it was so hard to be away from home. Sean snapped her out of her thoughts.

"You'd better start thinking about your outfits, Zoey. You're a fan favorite on the *Fashion Showdown Junior* website," Sean said. "So don't disappoint them or me! I want the two of us up there together at the finale, deal?"

"Deal," Zoey agreed with a smile. "Maybe I'll

sketch a little now, since we've got a few more hours."

"Many more hours," he corrected. "*Many.*"

As soon as the plane landed at the airport, and Zoey had deboarded, she fell into her father's arms. "I need a quick shower, and then take me to that baby!" she said.

Her dad and Marcus laughed and then assured her that was the plan. "Baby Melissa's been waiting to meet you, too," he said.

Zoey loved the way her father said "Melissa." "Is she adorable?" Zoey asked.

"Pretty darn cute," Marcus replied. "You're going to go nuts for her."

Marcus was right. As soon as Zoey saw Melissa in Lulu's arms, she was in love. The tiny fluttering hands, the button nose. Even the darks wisps of hair on her head were perfect.

"Can I hold her?" Zoey asked breathlessly.

"Oh, I *insist*," said Lulu. Her aunt seemed to have some kind of perma-smile on her face, which got bigger every time she looked at the baby. Zoey sat down on a chair, and Lulu carefully put the baby in Zoey's arms. Zoey couldn't believe how tiny and sweet-smelling Melissa was. Zoey kissed her forehead and then ran a fingertip across her little brow.

"Oh, Aunt Lulu, I just adore her!"

Lulu laughed. "She's adorable! John races home during his lunch hour just to see her, and your dad and Marcus come by almost every day. And you know, Essie helped me with laundry and things around the house. She was amazing."

Zoey smiled. She was starting to get used to the idea of Ms. Austen being a part of the family. Then Melissa made a tiny noise and then opened and closed her mouth.

"I think she might be ready for a feeding, Zo," Aunt Lulu said.

"Oh! Can I hold her a second longer, Aunt Lulu?" Zoey cried.

Zoey's aunt nodded. "But aren't you jet-lagged, honey?" she asked Zoey. "Maybe you should get some sleep."

Zoey nodded. "You're such a mom, already!" Zoey teased. "And yes, I should sleep. I have to get ready for the finale. They're shipping my four out-fits home so I can tweak them while I make the last two outfits. But honestly, I don't know how I'll ever do all that when I really just want to be here with you and Melissa!"

"You'll get it done," Lulu said. "You're a star, Zoey. Don't you know that by now?"

Zoey shook her head. "If being 'a star' means I try to fail and constantly doubt myself, well then, okay."

Lulu raised her brows. "Being 'a star' just means you keep on trying, no matter what."

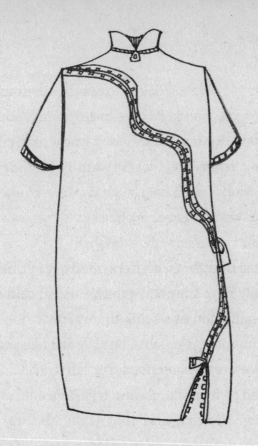

CHAPTER 12

Race to the Runway!

Wow. I thought the eight-hour challenges were hard. At least now I can post some sketches from the show. This is my Great Wall dress, in case you're curious!

But coming up with two runway-ready looks in just a few weeks—while catching up on schoolwork (again!), and being a very doting cousin to our family's new baby, *and* seeing my friends (for like five minutes), and you know, eating dinner and stuff—is practically impossible. Luckily, my friends are pitching in to help! They even made me flashcards to help study for some of my tests. Where would I be without my girls?

Back in the cafeteria with her friends, it felt like old times, only now Zoey had a new sense of calmness. Yes, she had a ton of sewing to do after school, not to mention math problems, but she felt like she had so much more perspective after her travels. She'd discovered that her family and friends would always be her top priority, and that while she was still completely devoted to being a designer, she wasn't going to miss out on any time with her friends or her fantastic new cousin.

"Did you see the photo series yet?" Libby asked, handing the school newspaper to Zoey.

Zoey shook her head. She knew Gabe had finished it because he'd sent her a draft of the article to read. He'd done a great job and had been very respectful of her privacy, as she'd known he would.

He'd also changed the focus to include Sean, which made her happy.

Just then Gabe came running over, red-faced. "I'm so sorry, Zoey," he said. "I checked the pictures to make sure, but I didn't notice the scarf. . . ."

"What do you mean?" Zoey asked. Confused, she flipped to the photo series page and saw the picture of her and Sean waving good-bye as they were about to leave for Tokyo. They were leaning against a sedan, and in the reflection of the car's window, you could plainly see the torso of a woman wearing a distinctive print scarf. The scarf Ms. Austen had been wearing nearly every day since Zoey had brought it back for her from Paris.

"Oh *noooo*," Zoey began. "Has anyone, uh, figured it out yet?"

Priti snorted. "You think *anyone* is going to figure out," she said, and then lowered her voice, "that your dad and Ms. Austen are together because of this picture? It would take Sherlock Holmes!"

Gabe shook his head regretfully. "Nope, just Emily. She noticed it and told me it was 'awfully weird' Ms. Austen was at your house as you were leaving. And then I think I might have turned red. . . . I'm so, so sorry, Zoey! She's going to tell the whole school in, like, five minutes."

Zoey let the news sink in. Would it be worse than having everyone see her being judged harshly on *Fashion Showdown Junior*? Worse than being teased by Emily? Suddenly, it didn't seem that bad. Ms. Austen was a popular principal and a nice person. She loved their school. And she seemed to love Zoey's dad, too.

"Well, so what?" Zoey announced, picking up her sandwich. "My dad can date anyone he wants. I'm just glad he has good taste."

Kate, Libby, and Priti cheered.

"Yes!" Priti shouted. "I wanted to tell you that to begin with! I didn't want you to think I was telling you how to feel."

"I love Ms. Austen," said Libby. "And look how great she was talking your dad into letting you go travel the world."

Gabe looked at Zoey hopefully, as if waiting to be officially forgiven.

"The photo series looks great, Gabe," Zoey said.

"Thanks for doing it. My dad will love it. I love it."

Gabe smiled with relief. "Thanks, Zoey. You're really . . . amazing."

At this, Zoey blushed and quickly bent her head to study the paper, hoping no one would notice her flaming cheeks.

When Zoey was home, she told her dad about the news, so he could warn Ms. Austen, but they weren't too concerned about the big secret coming out.

The students at Mapleton Prep, on the other hand, were more excited about Ms. Austen and Mr. Webber's dating life than they were about Zoey and Sean going to New York for the runway finale. Kids started saying Zoey was the principal's pet, but to Zoey's surprise, she didn't care. She knew enough about middle school at this point to know that some juicy new gossip would come along soon enough, and things would settle down. In the meantime she sewed her heart out, determined to show up to the finale with her absolute best work.

Soon, early on a Saturday morning, Zoey, Marcus, Mr. Webber—and Ms. Austen—left for New York. To her surprise, Zoey didn't really mind having Ms. Austen along. It was sort of nice to have another girl in the car, and it turned out that she and Ms. Austen had similar taste in music.

But first thing was first. Zoey had been waiting for this particular car ride ever since she returned from Shanghai. A few weeks ago she had received a package from Daphne Shaw, her fashion fairy godmother, with strict instructions to not open it until she was on the way to the runway show. It was one of the things that had kept her motivated over the last few days.

As soon as they were on the road, Zoey opened the card.

Dear Zoey,

Congratulations on making it to the finale! We are so proud of you, and we will be throwing a little party in your honor at the office after the show! Your father has all *the details . . . so see you soon, and "break a leg" on the runway!*

Daphne

Zoey looked at her dad. "You knew about this?"

"It's been in the works from day one," her dad said. "Isn't she sweet?"

Zoey was touched. Knowing that Daphne Shaw was supportive of her, win or lose, was just what she needed to calm her jitters.

When they arrived in the city, Zoey had to take her garments straight to the workroom so she could meet Anne-Thérèse and her other models to do any alterations. The runway show would be that evening, so there was very little time. Her family would do some sightseeing and then meet her at the taping.

Zoey was happy to find Sean already in the workroom, tailoring his two new outfits. Both were women's outfits, with a sportswear feel, and Zoey could see he was starting to discover his strengths as a designer.

"Those look great, Sean!" she said as she hung

up her two outfits. One was a wrap dress lined with a print so that when the model walked, the flap in the front would reveal the print on the inside. The other was a sleek, one-shouldered jumpsuit in a shiny eggplant-colored fabric, with printed trim on the pant cuffs and pockets. She'd labored over every seam on both outfits, so they were perfect.

"So beautiful!" Anne-Thérèse gasped when she saw the garments. They shared a warm hug.

Zoey said hello to the other contestants and models, chatting briefly with Cat and Leanne, but other than that, worked straight through the day, making sure all her outfits fit the models perfectly. She ignored the cameras as best she could.

When it was almost time to head out to the runway, Zoey went into the bathroom. She smoothed out her hair, retouched her lucky lip gloss, and took a deep breath.

This was it. She was sending out work she was proud of, competing against other top young designers, and she was ready.

Zoey found Sean on the way to the runway, and they clasped hands. "Good luck," he said.

"You too. I'm so glad we did this together!"

"Maybe we could open our own store someday," Sean said. "We could call it ZoSean or SeanZo."

"Deal," Zoey said. "But let's work on that name first, okay?"

When it was finally time for the runway show, Zoey was surprised to see a huge audience, but with all the lights, it was too bright to find her dad, Marcus, and Ms. Austen.

The runway show flew by. It was like Zoey blinked and it was over. Zoey could tell by the judges' faces how pleased they were with the quality of everyone's work. With only six contestants left, there didn't seem to be any one who stuck out as a clear winner or loser. They were simply *all* good.

While the judges decided the winner, an assistant ran to fetch Zoey's family so they could join her in the green room. To Zoey's surprise, he returned with not only her dad, brother, and Ms. Austen, but with Priti, Libby, Kate, Kate's mother, and Gabe!

"Oh my gosh!" Zoey cried. "What are you *all* doing here?"

Her friends surrounded her in a group hug, though Gabe held back, looking shy.

"Your collection was amazing, Zoey!" Priti squealed.

"*Sew* amazing," Libby added.

Kate tried to explain. "The producers invited friends and family to surprise you guys. My mom offered to bring us, and I invited Gabe, so he could take more pictures for his photo series."

Gabe blushed fiercely and then squared his shoulders. "That's not why—I mean—I wanted to cheer you on, Zoey. As your, um, friend. I hope that's okay."

"It's definitely okay," Zoey said. She had a feeling she knew what Gabe was trying to say. He was there because he really liked her. And the best part was, she really liked him too. She motioned at him to step aside. "Are you going to the party at Daphne Shaw's office later too?" she asked.

"Wouldn't miss it," Gabe told her. Then, to her surprise, he leaned in and gave her a quick, sweet kiss on the cheek. "Good luck, Zoey."

Now it was Zoey's turn to blush. Gabe was the

nicest guy she knew, and one of the most talented, and she realized she had really liked him for a really long time. And then she started smiling and couldn't stop.

Her thoughts were interrupted by an "ahem" from her dad and then an "ouch" when Ms. Austen nudged him.

"Shh, Jack, give them some space," Ms. Austen told Zoey's dad.

"Sorry, kids. My turn to congratulate her," said Mr. Webber as Gabe looked a bit sheepish. Then Mr. Webber put his arms around Zoey and squeezed. "I couldn't be more proud of you, Zoey."

Zoey squeezed him back. She was proud of her work too, whether or not it won. Ms. Austen, who'd also been hanging back slightly, came forward.

"Zoey," she said, pulling her to one side and speaking softly. "I just wanted to tell you I'm sorry if I came on a little too strong before. I was trying to be your friend, and maybe you're not ready to see me like that. It's just that I'm crazy about your father, and, well, I'm crazy about you, too. I've always wanted a daughter, and if I could pick any daughter in the world, it would be you!"

Zoey felt a flood of emotion. Ms. Austen loved her. And as much as Zoey had struggled with the idea of her father dating anyone seriously, especially the school principal, she had to face the reality that it looked like Ms. Austen might become a permanent part of their lives sometime soon. And her dad couldn't have chosen anyone better. She and Ms. Austen truly were cut from the same cloth.

Zoey reached out and took Ms. Austen's hand. "Thanks . . . *Essie*," she said, using her principal's first name for the very first time. "I'm glad you came this weekend. And I'm glad you're dating my dad."

Ms. Austen's eyes filled with tears, and she nodded, unable to speak. Zoey felt like she'd somehow just given her father permission to marry Ms. Austen, if that was what they wanted. She glanced over at Marcus, and he smiled at her, approving. Things in the Webber house were likely going to change soon. And Zoey was surprised to realize that she was actually excited at the possibility.

Zoey rejoined her friends and introduced them to Anne-Thérèse, whose parents had flown in for the finale. She could see Sean across the room with his parents, who were anxiously looking at the green light over the door, waiting for it to blink and signal that it was time for the results. Considering Sean's parents had had such a hard time letting him do the show, they looked awfully proud now. His father had his arm across Sean's shoulders, and his mother was beaming. Sean looked back at Zoey and grinned.

After what felt like an eternity, the green light began blinking. Zoey's family and friends took turns hugging her and wishing her luck. Marcus was the last to leave, and before he did, he said, "You're incredibly talented, Zoey. Mom would have been so proud of you. Good luck."

"Thanks, Marcus," Zoey replied, willing herself not to cry since she was heading straight to the contestants' seats. She took several big breaths and then followed the others out. As she sat down, she scanned the audience and found her family and friends waving at her. She smiled back and felt a sudden rush of calm. No matter what happened, she had all of them to go home with. She had a party at Daphne Shaw's office. She had more ideas, more projects, and more opportunities in her future. This was just one runway show in what would hopefully be a long career.

Oscar began to announce the judges' decisions. Leanne was dismissed, as was Maude and then Pia. Zoey held her breath, and next to her, she could hear Sean gasp a little. After a minute, to Zoey's disbelief, she and Sean and Cat were invited onstage to discuss their outfits with the judges. All three of them received praise and compliments for their ingenuity, and Zoey didn't know what to think. Did she dare to hope she might win?

Then Oscar announced a surprise: In addition to winning a year's supply of fabric and notions from a top fabric store and front-row tickets to the upcoming Fashion Week in New York, the winner's designs would be on the cover of and featured in an article in *Très Chic*.

Zoey's jaw dropped. It was more than she could have dreamed, and she suddenly wanted to win more than anything.

Zoey glanced out at her family again, and she

saw her father giving her a thumbs-up. Priti, Kate, Libby, and Gabe were all holding hands.

"Now, for the moment you've all been waiting for. All of you have done spectacular work throughout this challenge," said Oscar. "But there can only be one winning designer. One winner, who has shown a clear vision that is particularly unique and fresh. The winner of *Fashion Showdown Junior* is . . . Zoey Webber! Congratulations!"

A massive cloud of confetti came down, and through the haze of cheering and clapping, Zoey could hear one particular voice, her principal's, shouting over the din. "That's our girl!" Ms. Austen said. "That's our Zoey!"

Then Sean, who was still standing on stage, gave Zoey a big hug.

"Zoey, you did it!" Sean said with a huge grin. Then he whispered, "Go on, Zo. Oscar's waiting for you!" and gave her a nudge.

Zoey forced her legs to walk over to Oscar, who handed her a beautiful gold cup. "This is the first of many accolades," he said, "for the wonderful, talented, *Zoey Webber*."

Great stories are like great accessories: You can never have too many! Collect all the books in the Sew Zoey series:

Ready to Wear

On Pins and Needles

Lights, Camera, Fashion!

Stitches and Stones

Cute as a Button

A Tangled Thread

Knot Too Shabby!

Swatch Out!

A Change of Lace

Bursting
at the Seams

Clothes Minded

Dressed to Frill

Sewing in Circles

Cut From the
Same Cloth

If you liked

sewzoey

be sure to check out

these other series from

Simon Spotlight

IT TAKES TWO

If you like reading about
the adventures of
Zoey Webber, you'll love
Alex and Ava, stars of the
It Takes Two series!

A Whole
New Ball Game
by Belle Payton
1

Two Cool
For School
by Belle Payton
2

CUPCAKE DIARIES

Middle school can be hard . . .
some days you need a cupcake.

Katie and the cupcake cure

Mia in the mix

Emma on thin icing

Alexis and the perfect recipe

Katie, batter up!

Mia's baker's dozen

Emma all stirred up!

Alexis cool as a cupcake

Katie and the cupcake war

Mia's boiling point

Emma, smile and say "cupcake!"

Alexis gets frosted

CUPCAKE DIARIES — Katie's new recipe

CUPCAKE DIARIES — Mia a matter of taste

CUPCAKE DIARIES — Emma sugar and spice and everything nice

CUPCAKE DIARIES — Alexis and the missing ingredient

CUPCAKE DIARIES — Katie sprinkles + surprises

CUPCAKE DIARIES — Mia fashion plates and cupcakes

CUPCAKE DIARIES — Emma lights! camera! cupcakes!

CUPCAKE DIARIES — Alexis the icing on the cupcake

CUPCAKE DIARIES — Katie starting from scratch

CUPCAKE DIARIES — Mia's recipe for disaster

CUPCAKE DIARIES — Emma's not-so-sweet dilemma

CUPCAKE DIARIES — Alexis's cupcake cupid

CUPCAKE DIARIES — Katie sprinkled secrets

CUPCAKE DIARIES — Mia the way the cupcake crumbles

CUPCAKE DIARIES — Emma raining cats and dogs ... and cupcakes!

CUPCAKE DIARIES — Alexis cupcake crush